The Cowboy and His Mistletoe Kiss

Cowboys of Rock Springs, Texas #1

Kaci M. Rose

Five Little Roses Publishing

Copyright

Book Cover By: **Sweet 'N Spicy Designs**

Editing By: Debbe @ **On The Page, Author and PA Services**

Proofread By: Nicole @ **Southern Sweetheart Services**

Blurb

Dust off your boots and string the lights, Christmas has come to Rock Springs, Texas!

Lilly

Grateful to have a break from my trucking route, a casual visit to a friend completely altered my holiday plans. Stuck there by a surprise blizzard, I decided to make good use of my time and help prepare the ranch for the festivities to come. The fact that ranch hand, Mike, is hotter than a chestnut roasted on an open fire is just an added gift for me. As I listen to him talk about his plans and lofty goals, I find myself aching to meet him under the mistletoe. It would take a Christmas miracle to keep me off the open road, but one look at Mike, and I'm suddenly hoping Santa has one more trick up his sleeve.

Mike

Lilly was a surprise gift I didn't know I needed. For years, my goals have been focused on buying my own ranch to take in abused and neglected horses. Then, she blew in with the fresh, falling snow. Her life is on the road, and mine is rooted in Rock Springs. Can we find a way to turn a holiday fling into a lifetime of merry memories, or will our Christmas connection be stowed away with the tinsel and wreaths?

Come meet the small town of Rock Springs, Texas with a family that has your back, a town that knows your business, and men who love with everything they have.This is a Steamy, Small Town, Christmas Cowboy Romance. No Cliffhangers.This is Book 6 in the Rock Springs Texas Series.As always there is a satisfying Happy Ever After.If you love steamy Christmas romances with insta-love, hot love scenes, small towns, and cowboys, then this one is for you.

Dedication

To all those who make Christmas Magic possible for my kids. I hope they never stop believing in all the things the holiday can do.

Contents

Get Free Books!

Would you like some free cowboy books?
**If you join Kaci M. Rose's Newsletter you get books and bonus epilogues free!
Join Kaci M. Rose's newsletter and get your free books!**
https://www.kacirose.com/KMR-Newsletter

Now on to the story!

Prologue

Lilly

1 Year Ago

"Lilly!" I hear my name from a bubbly voice, the second I step out of my rig.

Riley.

The last time I saw this girl, she was covered in bruises and scared for her life. Now, she's smiling, outgoing, and beautiful.

I had no idea picking up a hitchhiker, in the middle of the night, would have such a huge impact on my life. Normally, they are just down on their luck or chasing a dream to be a movie star or music star. Not Riley.

She was running for her life and ended up right here with the love of her life, Blaze.

"Lilly," Blaze shakes my hand, and then catches me off guard, pulling me in for a hug. "Thank you so much for bringing my Riley to me and keeping her safe." There's a hitch in his voice that catches my attention.

I knew this would be an emotional day, and I was prepared, but having this big cowboy get so emotional on me, isn't something I was ready for.

"I'm so glad I did, and I'm glad it was me who crossed her path that night."

"Come on, Lilly. Let me introduce you to everyone." Riley hooks her arm in mine and leads me inside.

Walking in the kitchen door, I find eight more people, waiting to greet me, and I'm instantly overwhelmed. I grew up in a small house with just my mom, dad, and sister. Plus, trucking is a solitary job, and more often than not, I'm alone.

Riley introduces me to everyone, including Blaze's siblings, mom, dad, and a family friend.

They all talk at the same time asking questions, wanting to get to know me, and what happened that night I picked up Riley. Everyone is nice and friendly, but it's a lot to take in.

At one point before dinner, there's a lull in people talking to me, so I take the moment and slip outside the kitchen door for some fresh air. The warm Texas sun is starting to set, and the smell of hay and cows fill the air, and it immediately relaxes me.

In front of me, is a huge red barn, and it's bigger than any barn I've ever seen. From talking to Riley, I know this is the barn she hid in, the one Blaze and Sage found her in. As I near the barn, I take in the horses in their stalls, and other than their noise, it's pretty quiet.

The back barn doors are open, so I head down that way, checking out the pasture. There's a great view of the setting sun, so I sit on one of the hale bales to take it in.

My family is close, but nothing like Blaze's. They welcomed me into their lives just like that. They have truly accepted Riley, and now that she's engaged to Blaze, she will have the family I know she has been missing.

I've been feeling like something is missing lately. I know trucking isn't what I want to do my whole life, but what I want to do is a question I can't seem to answer.

The hay bale shifts with someone sitting down next to me, and when I look over, I find the most intense, brown eyes looking back at me.

"You must be Lilly." The deep, husky southern drawl washes over me, and I let my eyes take in the man beside me before I speak. He's all cowboy with wranglers, cowboy boots, and a flannel shirt. His tan skin shows he's not afraid of hard work, and there's just a hint of dark, brown hair peeking out from under his cowboy hat.

"Yes, I'm sorry. Am I in your way? I just needed some air." I start to get up, and he places a hand on my arm. I wasn't expecting the sparks and warmth from just one touch, and before I can stop myself, I jerk my arm away.

"Stay. I was just taking a minute to enjoy the sunset myself." He nods towards the pasture, where the sky is turning purple and orange.

"So, you're a truck driver?" He asks, his tone flat. I know where this is going. Because I'm a woman driving a rig, they make assumptions.

"Yes, it's a great way to travel." I'm partly joking. I love seeing the new areas, but you don't start driving a rig to travel. There's so much more to it than that.

"How did you decide to do that? Don't most girls want to be teachers or nurses?"

I look over at him, a bit shocked.

"Maybe where you come from, but I grew up right beside my dad fixing cars and trucks. He had a steady stream of truckers that he maintained their rigs for them, and they were always talking about their runs. It just hooked me."

"Still, that's not a job for a..."

"For a what?" I challenge him with a raised eyebrow. I know he's going to say a woman. I hear this more times than I can count. It was a great motivator, while I was learning.

When Dave gave me my first route, he took a chance on me, saying he always told his daughters they could do anything, so he needed to show them he believed it. That first year I put more miles on the books than any of the guys. The second year my truck broke down, and I fixed it myself and still made the delivery on time. That earned their respect.

"Well, you just seem too nice to be one of those rough truckers is all. How have they not chewed you up and spit you out?"

"You're judging that based on what? The less than ten minutes we've been sitting here together?"

"How many people would've stopped to pick up Riley, and then get her to safety? It's drilled into everyone's heads that you don't pick up hitchhikers."

"You'd be surprised how many would have stopped and picked her up. We tend to keep to ourselves and protect our own. Something I'm sure you're familiar with working here."

He nods but remains quiet. I'm not ready to head back inside, and something is drawing me to this cowboy.

"So, cowboy, what's your story? You seem to know mine."

"Mike," he says.

"What?"

"My name is Mike."

"Mike, cowboy, it's all the same."

The corner of his mouth tips up just a bit, but he keeps his eyes forward.

"I'm the senior ranch hand here. I grew up in Chicago, and I plan to have my own ranch one day, hopefully soon. I'd like to take in abused horses, rehab them, and then use them in a summer camp for kids."

I don't say anything at first. The idea is a good one, and he'll be helping horses and kids. What can I say to someone who knows what they want, when I have no clue?

"I think it's a great idea. I'm sure you've learned a lot here. From what Riley tells me,

Sage is pretty good with horses, and she's been teaching her a lot, too. Have you talked to Sage about working with her and learning what she knows?"

I feel his eyes on me, even before I turn my head and see them.

"You're going to fit in here just fine, Lilly. You should probably be heading back before they miss you."

I nod, stand up, and dust off my jeans, before turning to face him.

"Thank you for keeping me company." Then, I turn and go into the house for what I hope will be the first of many dinners here.

Chapter 1

Lilly

It's funny how this ranch is feeling more and more like home. After a scare, Riley's doctor put her on bed rest for the rest of her pregnancy. She begged me to come and keep her company on my days off the road, and of course, I said yes. Who wouldn't want to relax in the good, Texas countryside with some hot cowboy eye candy?

As I walk into her room, Riley's face lights up.

"Oh, thank you! I don't know why I'm craving ants on a log so much, because I haven't had it, since my parents were alive, but now, it's all I want to eat." She grabs the plate from my hands and starts eating, like she hasn't eaten in days.

"Well, that little one is going to rule your life for the next eighteen years at least, so you better get used to it," I joke.

I sit in the chair that her husband Blaze had brought in for those hanging out with Riley. It's crazy comfortable, and it even has heated and massage seats.

This room feels like Blaze and Riley. It's got reclaimed wood along the wall that the bed is on, but it's light and bright. The bed has a dark, brown leather headboard, and Riley softened it up with white sheets and off-white blankets, and even a lace throw.

There are pictures all over the room of Blaze and his family, and Riley added a few of her family, when she moved in. She also took the animal heads off the wall and replaced them with some old farm decor.

Some throw pillows and a few changes in furniture, and the place is no longer a bachelor pad, but a room I can see them both in. Riley has a great decorating eye, and she had so much fun redoing the room.

"So, are they in full on wedding planning mode down there?" Riley asks, while she snacks.

"Oh, yeah. They look so happy," I tell her.

Mac is Jason's younger brother. He and Sarah just got back from Mac's proposal at the lake house, and they want to be married just before Thanksgiving. In other words, in about three weeks from now. Being as they will be married here on the ranch, the date might work, but I know Riley is hating not being able to help. She has helped with everyone's wedding, and I can see it in her eyes that she wants to be involved here, too.

"Soon enough, this little one will be here, and you'll be back on your feet," I say, as I rub her belly. "Of course, only you would go and have a Christmas baby."

Riley and I both laughed when we found out she was due just days after Christmas. Talk about the best Christmas present that she could give us all.

She spent hours online, looking up all these super cute newborn Christmas photos that she wants to take when the baby is born. I think she's secretly adding to the list each day.

"Thank you again for coming, Lilly. I enjoy having you here."

"I like it, too. Wasn't ever a ranch person, but there's something about this place that calls to me. It's relaxing."

I don't tell her this ranch is starting to feel like home. I assume that's her plan to make me fall as in love with this place as she is.

Blaze walks in covered in dirt and grease. "I'm going to get cleaned up." He says, ducking into the bathroom.

"He and Mike have been fighting that tractor all morning, but I'll admit, there's something sexy about a man covered in grease," Riley says with her eyes on the bathroom door.

"Not happening, baby. You're on bed rest," Blaze yells from the bathroom.

Riley groans. "This sucks. Pregnant women shouldn't be put through this kind of torture."

Poor girl isn't allowed to have sex or even orgasms, while on bed rest, because the contractions can cause early labor. She has been complaining for days, and I always laugh. The laughing always earns me a glare from her. I guess I can't blame her. If I had a hot, cowboy husband, I'd want to ride him all the time, too.

Blaze steps out of the bathroom, looking at Riley with pure lust on his face. I want a man to look at me that way like I'm the only one he sees and the only thing that matters. I'm happy Riley has that, but I would be lying, if I didn't say I want it, too.

I stand up and give them their space when Blaze turns to me. "I know you're here for Riley, but would you mind heading down and giving Mike a hand with the tractor? If you can fix those rigs, you might be able to fix that old thing, too."

You can't run a big rig and not know how to fix one in a pinch. Plus, I grew up with my dad as a mechanic, so I learned a lot from him. It doesn't make me very popular with the guys when you can fix something they can't, but so far here on the ranch, that hasn't been an issue.

"What's wrong with it?" I ask.

"It's not starting. We checked the basics, but it's something a bit out of my scope." Blaze says as he sits down next to Riley.

Riley gets this smile on her face that I know means trouble. The last time she gave me that smile, I was sucked in as a food taster on the best recipe for Brussel sprouts. Yeah, there was no winner there. Now, I know that look means I need to hightail it out of there.

"Well, I think I'm going to take a nap. Why don't you go see if you can help him out?" Riley says.

I shake my head. I know what she's doing. She wants everyone to be as crazy in love as she is. It's not that I don't want to be in love, because I do, it's just impossible to find someone when you're on the road more than you are home. I've tried it and know from personal experience it just doesn't work. It works even less if you try to date another trucker.

I head downstairs, and Sarah greets me before my boots even hit the last step. She's full of smiles, as she takes my hand. We met when she got back to the ranch a week ago, but she has taken an instant liking to me. If I were to admit it, I like her, too.

I grew up a tomboy and didn't have too many girlfriends outside of my sister, so it's nice to have them now, all thanks to Riley.

Sarah has been in full on wedding planning mode since they got back from the lake house, and she has been all smiles about it, and involving anyone that walks by. Blaze's family owns the lake house in Walker Lake, Texas. I haven't been, but Riley has sent me pictures, and it's big enough for all five couples, Blaze's parents, and any future grandkids. It's right on the lake, and it's where Mac and Sarah met many years ago, and where they finally got together earlier this year. The family goes up a few times a year, taking some time away from the ranch.

"So, I have my wedding dress appointment next week. Did Riley tell you?"

"No."

"Well, she said you're to go in her place and have her on video call the whole time."

I laugh. "I wouldn't miss it."

Mac walks in the side door from the barn, shaking his head.

"Mike still struggling with that tractor?" I ask him.

"Yeah, told me to get out of his space with a few choice cuss words, so I left him to it," Mac cringes.

I can't help but laugh, deciding to go see what the big deal is.

Heading out to the barn, I take in the ranch. It's so peaceful here and full of life. I love coming here in between runs. What Riley doesn't know, is that right before she landed in the hospital, I sold my house in Tulsa, along with most of my furniture. I rented a small storage unit for the rest and picked up more routes to run, as they came up.

I've been with the company now for going on six years, so I have my pick of routes and stops. I don't want to drive a semi forever, and it's time to step up my game and save money to build my dream. What that is, I've still yet to discover. I just know it's not in Tulsa, not anymore.

My parents have moved on. They spend the summers in Montana, winters in Sedona, Arizona, and hardly ever make it back to Tulsa. I see them more when I have a route crossing their way. My sister got out of Tulsa the first chance she could and is now in Nashville singing. She's doing quite well; she always had an amazing voice.

So, being able to stay in Rock Springs, was perfect timing, and it was easy to scale down in order to spend time with Riley. I don't mind living out of my truck, but life on the road is pretty damn lonely.

Meeting someone wasn't on my radar much, until I watched Blaze's brothers fall in love one by one. Now I realize, what girl wouldn't want a sexy cowboy who looks at you like you hung the moon and the stars, treats you like gold, and loves you with everything he has?

"Goddamn piece of shit," I hear a gruff voice yell, and the sound of what I'm guessing is a wrench, hitting the concrete floor.

I walk into the barn and see Mike, kicking the tractor tire. His back muscles, rippling under his tight shirt, does something to my insides that I'm not quite ready to sort out just yet.

"Well, I wouldn't work for you either, if you treated me like that," I laugh, which earns me a glare. "Blaze sent me to help with the tractor."

"Took you long enough to get out here," he says, and I can see the tension in his muscles, as he crosses his arms, glaring at me.

"I'm here for Riley, and besides, it's been my experience that men don't like a woman coming in and showing them up."

"Well, I just want the damn tractor running, and I don't care if it's you, me, or Kit Kat, the damn horse, who fixes it," his voice raises.

I laugh, trying to ease some of the tension. Rolling up my sleeves, I go take a look. A minute later I can feel the heat of his body next to me. His arm brushes my side, and I feel like I've just been burned, even though the crisp fall air has a bit of a chill in it.

"Well?" He asks, his voice hoarse, or maybe, I'm imagining that.

"This is an easy fix," I tell him.

I get to work, and Mike hands me tools, as I ask for them. He watches what I'm doing and asks a few questions here and there. He's so close I can feel his body heat next to me. I try to force the thoughts away of how good his body feels next to mine, as I concentrate on the engine in front of me.

With my mind only half on the job in front of me, it takes double the time to fix than it should. A half-hour later the tractor is roaring to life, and Mike comes over, sweeping me up into a big hug.

"That's my girl!"

I've never had a guy so excited that I fixed something that he couldn't in my life. I've also never had a guy set my skin on fire, or make my heart race, when he's around like he does.

I'm in so much trouble.

Chapter 2

Mike

I can't seem to get Lilly off my mind. It's been a few days, since she helped me fix the tractor, and she has been in my thoughts every free second that I have.

When I first met her, I knew she was something special. She was hiding out in the back of the barn just like she is now.

She doesn't know I'm here yet, so I use the time to take her in. She has a rough exterior that I know has been built from her time on the road and growing up a tomboy, but on the inside, she's one of the nicest people I've ever met.

Her light, brown hair is pulled back with a few stray pieces framing her face. She has on her classic outfit of jeans and a dark, button-down flannel shirt over a tank top.

She's always willing to help and expects nothing in return, and around here, that's an amazing quality to have. It can also be dangerous with all the wedding planning going on. I hope she learns to say no, or who knows what she will get sucked into.

I've been on the ranch for almost six years now, and I remember the day Riley showed up. Then later, learning how Lilly helped Riley, and the family embraced Lilly at that first meal. It was overwhelming for her, so she took a breather and came out here for a few minutes, and that's how we met.

Just like that day, I sit down on the bale of hay beside her.

"What's on your mind, firecracker?" I watch her crack a smile at the nickname I gave her. She earned it the first time I saw her put one of the too handsy ranch hands in his place. I'm glad she never asked me about his black eye or my swollen knuckles the next day.

"It's just a bit much in there. I love how close they all are, but there are so many of them. Plus, weddings are very girly and not something I'm really used to." She shakes her head, staring out over the pasture.

"Never planned your wedding as a kid? Isn't that something little girls do?"

"That's what my sister did. She planned large elaborate weddings, and every once in a while, my mom would force me to join in and play with her. I was always in the garage with my dad covered in grease. The thought of having to stay clean enough to wear a white dress never appealed much to me."

"There's nothing wrong with that, and there's nothing wrong with needing a break either. I've been here six years, and I'm still not used to it. You just spent a whole day with the girls, and it's okay to need a few minutes to yourself."

I can tell by the way she won't look at me, and the way she's biting on her lip that she's feeling guilty about needing to take a break.

"You went wedding dress shopping today, right? Tell me about it." I ask, trying to take her mind off the path it's going down.

"Oh, you don't want to hear about that," she says, waving her hand at me.

"Maybe, I'm hiding too and could use the distraction."

Her eyes finally meet mine, and those intense, gray eyes steal my breath and make my heart race like they always do. I watch her take me in, and I can feel my body warm, as her eyes rake down my body. When her head turns to look back out at the pasture, it's like a cloud covered the sun and took its warmth away.

It's the same feeling I had the first time we sat out here. It's one I've never had before, and one I remember my dad describing to me that he would get, when my mom looked at him. He'd say they could be in a crowded room at one of his work events, and he just knew her eyes were on him because he could feel them.

I remind myself again about the ranch I'm looking to buy, and how I can't let anything get in my way. I've been working towards this dream for a decade now, and it's finally in my grasp. *No distractions.*

"We went to the same bridal store that all the other girls went to shop for their gowns. It was like tulle and chiffon had five hundred babies, and they all exploded in there."

I can't stop the laugh, which makes her laugh and shake her head, before she gives me a quick glance, and then looks away again.

"Sarah was glowing, and she loved trying on the dresses. Thankfully, she found what she wanted on her fourth dress. Riley had a blast being on video call, and the girl at the shop helping Sarah loved the idea. She then went on to pick out her bridesmaid dresses. You know, she asked me to be a bridesmaid? She just met me a week ago!"

"Well, they move fast in this family. I bet you're already on the top of her BFF list."

"I don't know if I find that funny, or if I'm horrified you know what BFF stands for," she laughs.

"Hey, I pay attention," I pause for a minute. "You know, you put on this hard shell, but it's a lot easier to see the woman inside than you think. I bet that's what she sees because it's what I see. You have this tomboy side that you think pushes everyone away, but under that, you're as much of a girly girl as the rest of them."

She sighs, and then turns to look at me again, "You think you have me all figured out?"

I just shrug. I wish I did, but there are so many sides to Lilly that I can't wait to see if she will let me in long enough to discover them. Then, I have to remind myself again, no distractions, and figuring Lilly out, is a major distraction.

Besides, she's just visiting and doesn't live here, and getting involved with someone that doesn't have roots in Rock Springs, isn't possible when I'm looking to buy a ranch here.

"Enough about me. Any new plans on your ranch?"

I took this job on the ranch to work and save up money to buy my own ranch. So many times, when I tell people about my idea, their first response is to laugh. A city kid from Chicago owning a ranch, they say. Yeah, my dad is a big businessman in Chicago, and my mom is a society woman who loves to volunteer. They are amazing people and taught me to always help someone when I can.

My parents have been nothing but supportive of my dream to own the ranch, and my dad made me a deal. If I got a job as a ranch hand for five years, saved up money to buy the ranch, and gained the experience, then he'd buy my first several horses and cover their costs for the first year.

When I told Lilly of my plan, I waited for the laughing, but it never came. Her first question was if I had talked to Sage to ask about working with her and rehabilitating the horses. I was shocked speechless that she was interested, and never once, thought I couldn't do it. She has been my biggest cheerleader, besides my parents, ever since.

"Well, I'm at the point of starting to look for places. For years, I always said I didn't care where the ranch was, but now, I know I want to stay in this area, and as close to Rock Springs as I can. That limits my possibilities quite a bit."

"Don't settle. You'll find the perfect place. Since you will be doing a summer camp, you want different things for the kids to do. A place that has a swimming hole would be perfect in the Texas summer heat."

"I know, but it's the being patient part. The day I hit my five year anniversary here and met my father's requirements, I started looking. He sends me places closer to Chicago all the time, so I started sending him back ads for open office spaces in Dallas."

She laughs, "How did he take that?"

"He told me to convince my mom to allow him to open a Dallas branch, instead of retiring, and he'd do it. I have yet to have that talk with her."

"You might have a better chance of convincing your parents to move to your ranch and help with the horses," she jokes.

"I might." I smile at her.

"I better get back in there, before they realize I'm missing. I'm sure there's tulle to fluff or something that needs glitter."

"Well, I'm available for rescue service any time, just send the signal." If only she knew how much I really would love to spend any amount of time with her.

"Ahhh, Lilly. There you are," Mac says, catching us both off guard. "They're assigning wedding duties, and trust me, you don't want them to pick for you."

"Yeah, no. I'm going to head back." She turns to look at me, placing her hand on my shoulder, "Thanks for keeping me company." Her hand trails off my shoulder, as she walks away. If Mac wasn't standing in front of me, I know I'd be following her back to the house and subject myself to all things wedding planning, just for a little more time.

When my eyes turn back to Mac, I find him watching me, and I'm sure I've been caught staring after her.

"I didn't see it before, but maybe, Riley and Sarah are on to something," Mac says, shaking his head with a smile on his face.

"What in the devil are you talking about?"

"Well, Riley and Sarah have been talking about Lilly. Sarah asked her to be a bridesmaid, and I'm here to ask you to be a groomsman."

"What?"

"I think there's some matchmaking going on if I know the girls. I think they're trying to set you two up."

Walking down the aisle with Lilly, and dinner and dancing at the reception? Oh, this smells like Riley for sure, but I'd be stupid to pass up the opportunity for any amount of time with her.

One night with her, on a day I'd planned to take off anyway, isn't a distraction, right? It's just the company of a friend who is going to the same event.

"I'm assuming they have plans to pair me with Lilly?" I ask.

"Yep. Sarah has more bridesmaids than I have friends as it is. I asked Mo, the chief from the reservation I grew up on, to be a groomsman. He's being paired with Sarah's friend Jenna. Sarah insisted on me asking Ben as well. She thinks there might be something with him and Sky. She wouldn't listen when I said there wasn't. Now, they have their matchmaking eyes set on you. So, I can tell Sarah you'll do it, right?"

"Yes, of course."

Mac slaps his hand on my back, before turning to walk back to the house. "May God have mercy on your soul with those two. You will need it."

Don't I know it.

Chapter 3
Lilly

One thing I have noticed with truckers is we travel to all parts of the country, but if you ask each one, they have an area of the country they like best. For me, it's out west, where the road isn't flat. I like seeing the mountains, and I don't mind driving through them.

I don't enjoy driving out east, like the run I just did from Dallas to Atlanta and back. It was all flat land with some hills. The most interesting things to see are the billboards. Every town looks the same, and every state blurs together.

I'm happy to be back on the ranch, and if I'm honest, I'm happy they let me sleep in today as well. My hours on the road are early pickups and driving at night, when the traffic is minimal.

When I get downstairs, the house is empty and quiet. With no one here, it actually feels as big as it looks. This house is massive, even by Texas standards. Ten people are living here right now, eleven when I'm here, and you would never know it. With everyone inside, the place feels cozy and like home. There's plenty of room to spread out and have privacy, but there's always someone around when you need it.

With everyone out, the house feels big and empty, kind of like how my house in Tulsa started to feel. I had no one there to help make the place feel like home, and when I started to dread going home, I knew it was time. Best choice I ever made.

Before coming downstairs, I check on Riley, and she's napping and out like a log. She has been doing a lot of sleeping, and I don't blame her. I would, too. I can only imagine how much energy it takes to produce another human.

I grab a muffin off the counter, as I head outside to see what everyone is up, too. I hear Sage in the horse pen to the side of the barn, so I follow the sounds of the clopping of the horse's hoofs on the dirt.

I climb up on the metal fence and sit on the top, as it squeaks under me. Sage has a small barrel racing course set up in a pen and is walking Kit Kat around the three barrels.

"What're you doing?" I ask her.

"I was watching her the other day, and I think she'll be a great barrel racing horse. I had some time today, so I figured I'd set up a small course, get her used to the barrels, and see how she does."

"You ever barrel raced before?" I ask her.

I've been to many rodeos, and it always amazes me the dedication and relationship those that compete have with their animals. I could easily see Sage competing.

"It's been a long time, but I'm not looking to do it as a career. Just to go out, make some connections, and get my name out there for new clients. It could help Mike too now that he's looking for his place."

At the mention of Mike, my heart races a bit, and I have to take a deep breath. He was on my mind the whole time I was on the road. I'd be lying if I said I wasn't excited to see him again. I got in last night and went straight to bed, so we haven't run into each other.

While I was on the road, I did a lot of thinking. Was I excited to get back to Rock Springs for Riley and the town, or was it because of Mike? I don't want to make a huge decision like putting down roots here based on a guy. The fact I can't answer that question has me a bit worried.

"Did you check on Riley, before you came out?" Sage asks.

"Yeah, she was sleeping."

Sage chuckles, "She needs the rest. Okay, let's see what this girl can do."

She hops up in the saddle and rides Kit Kat around the barrels in what looks like a crisscross triangle pattern. She does great, and with each pass, Sage picks up speed. After ten or so rounds, she comes to a stop in front of me.

"I think she's ready for a real track. I'll have to get one set up in the field. If I do it myself, Colt will get mad, so I need to talk to him."

Colt has this need to protect Sage, and he loves to spoil her. So, I know tomorrow he will have everyone working on the barrel course, and it will be completed by dinner.

Sage walks Kit Kat around once more, and I'm so mesmerized by how much Kit Kat trusts Sage that I don't hear anyone walking up until the fence shakes. Mike sits down beside me, and Colt and Blaze stand on the other side of him.

"Hey, guys!" Sage calls to them.

"She ready for a real course?" Colt asks.

Sage smiles, and it's one that's reserved only for Colt. "She is."

"I'll get on it then." Colt doesn't even hesitate.

"Hey, so I got a call from the sheriff," Blaze says, and we all turn to look at him. "There has been talk about an illegal rodeo in the area."

"What does that mean?" I ask.

"Well, generally the horses are stolen, drugged, and pushed to their limits. When they're no longer useful, then they kill them. They run them for high stakes betting and other illegal gambling. It's been a while since there have been any up this way." Colt says.

I can't help but cringe, as he talks about how the horses are treated. How are people so heartless to treat an animal like that? One who gives you their trust. I watch Kit Kat the way he trusts Sage, and my heart bleeds for the animals they are torturing.

"The sheriff knows you take in stray and abandoned horses, Sage. So, he wants you to keep an eye out and an ear to the ground, and if you hear anything, let him know," Blaze says. "I'm going to head in and check on Riley. Let's not worry her with this right now."

We all agree as he goes into the house.

Mike jumps down from the fence, and his large hands wrap around my waist, as he helps me down as well. His moves are slow, and his eyes are on mine. The air between us crackles, and time seems to stop. Before I can put my finger on what changed, my phone rings.

It's Dave, my boss.

I offer Mike a small smile before I answer the phone.

"Hey, Dave. Got another run for me?"

"Yes and no." His burly voice answers.

"What does that mean?"

"I have a run for you right before Thanksgiving, and you'll be back in time to celebrate. Also, I was looking at your hours and all, and because you're one of my best employees, I need you to take some time off. Use vacation leave and relax a bit."

"Dave, I'm plenty relaxed."

"When was the last time you took time off or even took a vacation?"

"I don't know, but I'm sure you'll tell me." I huff, as I rack my brain for the dates of my last vacation.

Was it when I helped Mom and Dad move to Montana? That was five years ago. I know I've taken time off since then. I've slowed down, since coming to help Riley out, and that has to count for something, right?

"Three years ago, and you put in for a five-day weekend, Lilly."

Oh, that's right. It was to go see one of my sister's concerts. Was that three years ago?

"Well, I've slowed down recently, and I've been spending more time here in Rock Springs."

"Yes, but you still message me daily about your next route. You have more miles on the books than anyone, and because I care, I'm ordering you to take some time off for your health. Do this run, and then take the week after Thanksgiving to relax. Don't think of work, and just take it easy. Maybe, visit a spa, get a massage, or get wrapped in whatever plant is trendy right now."

I chuckle. "Dave, I don't do spas, but I respect you, so I'll take a week and relax the best I can, I promise. I'll even send you some pictures as proof. Deal?"

"Deal. Now, I know you have the wedding coming up, so relax a little there too and have fun."

"Not likely, but I'll try."

"Try hard, Lilly. See you in a few days. "

After we hang up, I notice Mike watching me.

"Everything okay?" He asks.

"Yeah, that was my boss. He has a run for me after the wedding. I'll be back for Thanksgiving, but then, he's making me take some time off."

"Really? I thought he wanted you to work more during Christmas."

"He does, but he noticed that I hadn't taken time off in three years, so he's ordering me to take a week before things pick up too much."

"Wow, I thought I was a workaholic. At least, I make it back to see my parents every year."

I shove his shoulder. "I see my parents several times a year, whenever I'm in the area. We always have dinner together or more, if I have time."

"What did you do on your last vacation?"

"My sister is a country singer, and she's pretty good. I know my opinion is biased, but she is. She had a charity event concert, so Mom, Dad, and I went out to support her. It was a weekend festival, and we had fun. I didn't realize that was the last time I took time off."

"Sounds like your boss is looking out for you."

If I didn't know better, I'd say there was a hint of jealousy in his voice. But that can't be right, can it?

"I think it's more like his wife is. She handles all the books, probably noticed it, and then told him."

He nods and then turns towards the house. "Well, let's head in. You need to tell Riley you'll be leaving after the wedding."

Chapter 4

Lilly

"It's not burgundy, it's wine," Riley tells me again. She's talking about the deep red color of the bridesmaid dress I have on. Sarah's getting married today, and we are all getting ready in Sage's room in the main house.

It's the master bedroom with high ceilings, a large fireplace, and exposed wood beams, and it's a showstopper. Megan is doing Sarah's hair with some of her supplies from the beauty shop she owns in town.

"I'm sorry both colors look the same to me." I try to mean the apology. I'm sitting in the chair next to Riley, who is propped up on the couch per Blaze's orders.

The dress isn't bad. I love the color and the lace on the top. It's also long and flowy at the bottom and more comfortable than I expected it to be.

Riley looks me over and smiles. "You're doing really well. I know this isn't your thing, and it's a bit much for you. There's time if you want to go for a short walk."

After I disappeared the first night I came for dinner, Riley saw me coming back in and pulled me to the side. She wanted to make sure everything was alright, so I decided to be honest with her and tell her everything, and that I was a bit overwhelmed. She completely understood and has been very supportive ever since.

I sigh, "Thank you. I'll have my phone, but I just need a minute."

I grab the jean jacket that we're wearing over our dresses, because it's late November in north Texas. I walk downstairs to the kitchen and get a drink of water, as I stare out of the kitchen window, thinking about Mike. I will be walking down the aisle with him today, and we'll be pushed together at the reception.

I know Riley and Sarah planned this because I heard them talking. I hope it will help me understand better of whether I want to be in Rock Springs for him, or because I truly love the area.

Mike makes me feel things I've never felt before, but I know it won't work. I've tried dating, while I've been on the road, and it never works out. Either they don't trust that I'm not cheating on them, or they need to call me constantly to know I'm okay. Oh, my favorite is when they say I spend too much time on the road, even when I slow things down, while we're dating.

I'm lost in thought, when a throat clears behind me, making me jump.

I turn to see Mike done up in his wedding attire. He's in dark jeans, boots, a long white sleeve button-up shirt, and a brown suede vest. He has his cowboy hat in his hand, and the sight steals my breath. His muscles stand out, and a shiver runs through me, as I think of those strong muscular arms wrapped around me the other day, as he helped me down from the fence.

His hands clench his hat even tighter, as his eyes roam my body, and then meet mine.

He clears his throat, "You look stunning, Lilly."

I can feel the heat cover my face, but I still can't help but smile.

"You look pretty good there yourself, cowboy."

His smile grows even wider before he nods to the door. "Want to go for a quick walk?"

I had planned to step outside to clear my head, not cloud it even more, before the wedding. But I do want some more time with him, so I look at my phone, seeing nothing from Riley. We still have half an hour, before the photos. "Yeah, I need some air anyway."

He opens the kitchen door and follows out behind me. He walks beside me, as we walk across the yard to the barn.

As we enter the barn, the shade gives the air a nice chill, so I go to put my jacket on, but Mike takes the jacket from me, holding it open for me to put on. His hands brush my shoulders, and it almost feels intentional. The warmth of his touch spreads down my arms, catching me off guard, yet again.

"Thank you," I murmur, as I step away. Megan has done my hair and makeup, and I have a feeling that if I kiss him like I want to, then it will mess up all that hard work. So, I try to keep a good amount of space between us as we walk.

"There have been a lot of weddings here this year. Several of us think you started all that," Mike smiles.

"What do you mean?"

"Well, you brought Riley to us, causing Blaze to fall head over boots. That caused

Sage and Megan to both see what was right in front of them. Sage getting married brought Ella to Jason, and their honeymoon brought Mac and Sarah together."

"All because I did what my mom yells at me not to do. I have a soft spot for women stranded on the road," I smile. I soak in the smell of hay and wood. It's a combination that I wish I could carry with me in my rig on my long hauls.

I stop in front of Kit Kat, the horse who has been watching us walk, and pet her. She's a very loving horse, more than the others. She's been spoiled by the girls on the ranch, so she's friendlier and secretly my favorite.

Mike reaches over and gives her a treat like it's no big deal. Like he isn't an inch away from me, and like I can't feel the heat of his body, soaking into mine.

He looks over at me with what looks like desire in his eyes. As he pulls his hand back from Kit Kat, it brushes against my arm, when I have reached out to pet her. I soak in his touch for just a moment, before I pull back, clearing my throat.

"You know this is probably the most spoiled horse in history, and you men spoil her just as bad as the women do," I give him a pointed look.

"It's the eyes. She looks at you, and you can't tell her no." His voice is a bit huskier than normal, and I hope I have the same effect on him that he seems to have on me.

I laugh, "Come on. We need to head back before they send out a search party."

We take our time enjoying the fall air, as we go back to the house. The calm from our walk is broken the second we step inside, and the flurry of wedding preparations hits us. The guys are getting ready to head out to the church, so we can get our pictures done.

"Well, I'll see you at the church," Mike winks at me before I go back upstairs.

• • • • • • • • • •

"Just one dance!" Riley pouts at Blaze.

"No, you're supposed to be on bed rest with your feet up. Doctor's orders."

"It's a wedding, Blaze! I want to celebrate with Mac and Sarah. One dance."

"Nope. Wait, what're you doing?" Blaze's eyes go big, as he watches Riley pull out her phone.

"I'm calling the doctor, and if she says yes, you have to dance with me."

They are so darn cute. Mac and Sarah's reception has such a great energy to it, and I can't blame the girl for wanting to dance. I make my way to the bar to refill my drink when Mike steps in front of me.

My heart skips a beat, as I remember walking down the aisle with him pressed to my side. Then, having him standing next to me for the whole ceremony, since Sarah had the couples stand together, instead of doing girls on one side and guys on the other. He kept his hand on top of mine, rubbing circles with his thumb the whole time. It was all my mind could focus on, and I don't remember a detail about the ceremony.

"Dance with me." It's not a question. Mike is not giving me a chance to say no, as he takes my hand, leading me on to the dance floor.

His hand rests on my waist, and his other hand takes mine, pulling me close. I rest my hand on his shoulder, and he sways to the music.

"Is it a cowboy rule that you have to know how to spin a girl around the dance floor?" I ask, watching the other couples.

"It might be. I don't think I've met a cowboy who can't dance. It's a great way to impress the ladies."

"Oh, is it now?"

"Let me ask you, are you impressed by my dancing skills?"

Was I? Yes, but would I full on admit that to him? *No.* So, I give him a small grin and act like I'm thinking about it.

"Well, you haven't stepped on my feet, so that's a plus."

The song ends, and a slower one fills the speakers. Mike pulls me in until his chest is against mine, and he whispers in my ear.

"What about now?"

"I can see the possibilities," I say, more breathless than I meant, too. His head rests against mine, and he starts singing the song to me, as my stomach flutters. Could he mean the words that he's falling for me and hopes I feel the same way?

The next song is a bit faster, so he puts more space between us, but the look on his face is intense like he's holding himself back.

I clear my throat, trying to pull us from this lust fog.

"Your parents get into town tonight, right?" I ask.

He stares at me a minute more, before he nods, "Yeah, they're going to do dinner in Dallas, and then head out here. Sage insisted they have Thanksgiving here with all of us, and they jumped at the chance for a real southern Thanksgiving, as my mom puts it."

"What's so different about a southern Thanksgiving?"

"Up north, we don't brine our turkeys in sweet tea, we don't put bacon in our green beans, collard greens don't have a place on a Thanksgiving table, and we do yeast rolls, not biscuits."

"Remind me never to have Thanksgiving above the Mason Dixon Line then." I give a fake shutter, causing him to laugh. "Though now, I can't wait to watch your parents take it all in."

The song ends, and I step back, "I'm going to get some water." I turn and head towards the bar, before Mike can answer. I order water and keep my back to the dance floor for a minute, while I try to recompose myself.

When I turn around, I scan the crowd. In the middle of the dance floor, are Mac and Sarah with smiles so big and eyes just for each other. I catch Mike out of the side of my eye, and my heart races.

He's not just dancing with someone else, but he's dancing with the flower girl. She's the daughter of one of the ranch hands and can't be more than eight-years-old. He's showing her how to dance, and the smile on his face is huge. Finally, he picks her up and sets her feet on top of his feet, so they can glide around the dance floor.

The smile on the girl's face is big, and I know she will remember this moment for a long time. I can't help but to think of what a great dad he will be, dancing with his daughters and showing them how they should be treated. What fun it will be for his kids to grow up on his ranch, working with the horses each day and meeting new friends every summer.

In the next moment, I'm picturing me by his side, helping him on the ranch, and our kids running in the front yard. Crap, spending time with him isn't helping. Maybe, this run will give us a bit of distance we need.

Chapter 5

Lilly

I'm walking into some mom and pop Tex-Mex restaurant when the smells of salsa and taco meat fill the air. The bright neon colors on the walls and decor are meant to cheer the place up, and they do bring a small smile to my face.

I even laugh at the *Welcome to Your Taco Dealer* sign, before I spot my mom, waving from the back corner to get my attention. I smile, wave back, and make my way over to my parents.

When I called my parents and said I had a stop in Flagstaff, they insisted on driving up for dinner, and of course, there was some new place they wanted to check out, so here we are.

"Lilly baby, look at you. That time on the ranch is doing wonders for your skin! What is in the Texas water? I need you to bottle it up and send me some," Mom gushes, as she hugs me tight.

"Hey there, tiger," Dad says, pulling me into a hug next.

"You pick up a new route? It's been a while since you've been out this way." Mom asks once we are seated.

"Yeah, I've been spending time in Rock Springs with Riley, and this route was from Dallas to San Diego and back. I've been gone about a week and will get home in time for Thanksgiving. Dave is forcing me to take vacation time after that because I haven't used any in a few years."

"Well, he's right. You do need time off, even if you don't realize it. Have you thought more about what you want to do?" Mom digs right into what she wants to know.

My parents know I sold my place in Tulsa, and I've been trying to find a home with the goal of eventually getting out of trucking. My sister only knows I sold my place. She's so busy right now, and I didn't want to bog her down with the details.

"I don't know. I like Rock Springs, and I have friends there, but I'm not sure what I'd do. Sage has been looking for help with the horses now that Riley is on bed rest and will soon have a baby. I've been watching her and learning some from her."

"You always had a fascination for horses and animals," Dad agrees.

"And engines," Mom adds.

My parents always supported me going into trucking, even though my mom would have had me do just about anything else. My dad has not hidden the fact that he loves how I can hold my own with the truckers, and I know he gets satisfaction when I can fix something a guy can't, even though he will never admit it.

As a teenager, I would help in his shop after school. Any time one of the guys was having problems with something, instead of fixing it himself, which would be easier, he would tell the guys to let me have a look. Nine times out of ten, I fixed it. When I couldn't, I loved the times Dad would crawl under the hood with me and teach me something new.

I miss those days, but I know he was happy when he sold the shop to one of the guys who had been with him from the start. I'm happy for him and Mom to retire.

After we order, Mom turns to me and starts in on the cowboys again. Since they moved to Montana in the summers, she has a bit of an obsession with them.

"So, tell me about this Rock Springs," Mom places her hands under her chin, leaning forward on her elbows.

"You know about Riley and Blaze. She's on bed rest right now and asked me to come and keep her company between runs. I like the ranch. It's peaceful, and there's always something to do. The town is friendly, and I know, because I've been doing runs there for years. They will have a true southern Thanksgiving at the ranch, and Mac and Sarah even postponed their honeymoon to be around for the meal. Then, they'll head out for their honeymoon."

"Are there any single cowboys that have caught your eye?" Mom pries and my mind goes right to Mike. There's nothing there and no reason to send her down that rabbit hole.

I sigh, "Not really, but if they do, you'll be the first to know. Have you heard from Vanna?" I try to change the subject.

My sister Savannah started singing after she got out of an abusive relationship. She turned it into a song, and it landed her a record deal. She loves songwriting and just put out an album in Nashville, which has been gaining some popularity.

She's the reason I was so glad to help Riley because I wasn't there to help Vanna. If it weren't for the kindness of a stranger, who knows where Vanna would be today.

"Oh yes, she called last night. She got asked to open on a big tour that's going up the east coast, starting in March. She's really excited. I looked the band up, and it should be some good exposure for her. They're also involving her in some of the hype and interviews," Mom goes on, like a proud mama bear.

"That's good. She's been working hard on that album. I might try to take a route out that way and catch a show or two."

"Oh! We could meet you there to show some family support! Just let us know when and where." Mom gushes, as Dad stays silent, but nods his head in agreement.

"I will, Mom."

"Now, tell us about this wedding! You know, in Montana country weddings in barns are all the rage. They've made a whole business out of event barns! Who knew?" Mom waves her hands in the air and laughs.

"Well, they do have an event barn on the ranch. It was the original barn from what I understand. They didn't want to tear it down, so they repurposed it. Although, it's just for family, friends, and such, and they don't rent it out. They have auctions and events on the ranch each year. All the wedding receptions have been held there as well." I go on to tell them about the ranch church and the decor, and even about Nick's amazing food at the reception.

The rest of the dinner is uneventful just catching up and talking shop. They ask about the people of Rock Springs as if they have lived there and know everyone.

After dinner, I head back to my hotel, since I can't pick up the next load, until morning. My phone rings just as I'm getting in.

"Hey, firecracker," Mike's husky voice fills my ear and turns me inside out, using a nickname that should irritate me. This is the first time he's called me, while I've been out on the road, so a second later, I start to worry.

"Is everyone okay? Is Riley okay?"

"Whoa, yes. Why would something be wrong?"

"Because you never call me," I tell him.

"Ahhh, well we have a ranch truck that needs some of your love when you get back, but I just wanted to see how you're doing. I know you said you'd be having dinner with your parents tonight."

"You remembered that?"

The line goes quiet, and I pull the phone away from my ear to see if we are still connected, and we are.

"Mike?"

"Lilly, I pay attention to what those I care about say, and you fall in that category. You're one of us on this ranch, and Riley sees you as family. If you haven't figured out her whole reason for asking you to come help her was to make you fall in love with this place, so you move here, then let me tell you, it is. Every one of them sees you as family, and they'll treat you that way. I'm here too, and I'd like to think we're friends, which I think is a good place to start."

Start? Does he mean he wants more? Does he like me as more than a friend? Does he want to ask me out? Do I want him, too?

Listen to me, I'm worse than those girls in school I'd hear whispering about boys in the school bathroom.

"We're friends, and I know Riley wants me to stay. She has been not so subtly hinting at it and trying to bribe me."

"Is it working?"

"Well, if you can keep a secret, I'll tell you. But I mean it, you'll be the only one on the ranch who knows."

"Who am I going to tell other than Kit Kat?"

I laugh because that horse is the star of the ranch. She was born right before Jason and Ella got married and has soaked up everyone's love and attention. Basically, she's one spoiled horse.

"I sold my place in Tulsa."

"What? Why?"

"I did it before Riley was put on bed rest. It's not home anymore. My sister is getting ready to go on tour, and my parents don't live there. I got into trucking to get out of there. So, I sold it and put my stuff in storage, and I've been living in my truck and now the ranch."

He's quiet for a minute again, like he's trying to pick his words. "Any plans to put down roots anywhere?"

"It's the plan, but where I don't know. I was picking up extra runs to save money, but I've cut back down again when Riley called. Now, Dave is making me take a vacation, so I'm glad to be at the ranch."

"You work too hard."

"Says the man whose last vacation was when?"

"Point taken."

I settle down on the bed and realize talking with Mike is easy. There are no awkward silences, and I'm not at a loss of what to say. Normally, I have to watch my every word around a guy, because heaven forbid, I show him up. With Mike, I feel like he dares me to prove him wrong.

"We both have goals, Mike, and there's nothing wrong with working and giving our all to achieve those goals."

"What's your goal then, Lilly?"

"I'll let you know when I figure it out."

"Will you be at the ranch, when we decorate for Christmas? If you are, you'll be glad to be there, because it's a sight to be seen."

"Yeah, that's what Sage told me. I guess, she's a bit Christmas obsessed."

"Oh, she is, and even has a Christmas themed guest room," Mike laughs.

I remember hearing talk about that, and I make a mental note to go in search of it when I get back to the ranch.

We talk for a little longer about what's going on at the ranch before I have to fight back a yawn.

"I hate to cut the conversation short, but I have an early pick up tomorrow and really need to get to bed."

"Of course, you get some sleep and be safe, firecracker. I'll see you in a few days."

Lord, help me survive the next week around that man.

Chapter 6

Mike

I'm usually the first one up and in the barn for the day, being the senior ranch hand it's up to me to make sure everything is done that needs to be done. Colt will normally leave me a list from the day before on anything out of the normal that's left to do.

I'm going over my own list in my head and stop in my tracks when I hear metal clinking coming from the other side of the barn. I make my way over to the ranch truck that has been running hard and find legs sticking out from under the truck.

I'd recognize those legs and boots anywhere. *Lilly.*

I lean against the barn and take her in. Her jeans hug every curve on her legs, and I can't help but think about those legs wrapped around my waist. I feel the flush crawl up my neck at the thought, and my hands ache to grab hold of the perfect globes of her ass that the jeans she wears showcase so well.

I'm getting hard at the thought, so I know it's time to stop and make myself known. I take a deep, calming breath, before clearing my throat. The noise stops, and Lilly slides out with just a tank top on. She makes no move to sit up from the mechanic's creeper that we keep to work on trucks and tractors.

"Well, you going to stand there like a stalker, or are you going to help me? Hand me that blue ratchet extender," Lilly says, as she points to the tool just out of her reach.

I walk over, crouch down next to her, and then do as she asks.

"How long you been out here?" I ask her.

"Since sunup. This last haul messed with my sleep schedule, so I figured there's no point in fighting it with work to be done around here."

"So, my dad called me last night," I rub the back of my neck, as I bring the subject up.

"Yeah? Is everything okay?"

"Uh, huh. They booked a room at the bed and breakfast in town for Thanksgiving and also found two ranches for us to go look at, while they're here."

The noise stops again, and she slides back out to look at me.

"Did you look at those places yet?"

"No, they're out of what I'm comfortable paying."

"Don't let them talk you into something that isn't right, or that will stress you out each month to make the payments."

I shake my head, "I think my parents are just ready to call me a ranch owner, instead of a ranch hand. They expected me to buy a place last year. You know, this is the first time they'll be in Rock Springs."

"They haven't visited you before?"

"Nah, I always go home for the holidays, when I can."

She gives me a side eye and slides back under the truck, "Why now?"

"My dad is only working two days a week, and my mom has resigned from a few of her board spots. In other words, they're starting to retire."

"Think they'll move out here to be near you?"

"I don't know. They're city born and raised, but stranger things have happened."

We both laugh, and then work in silence for the next half an hour, before Lilly slides back out, nodding towards the truck. "Start her up."

I open the creaky truck door and crank the key. The truck roars to life, and the engine sounds better than it has in a long time.

"I don't think she has sounded that good, since she rolled on to the ranch," I shake my head.

"Well, you can cross that off your list for today. What else needs to be done?" Lilly stands up, dusting her jeans off.

"Let's see. Today, we're pulling out all of the Christmas stuff, and then decorating outside and the barn. The inside gets done after Thanksgiving."

She nods and looks up at the house. "Well, let me go get cleaned up, and I'll be out to help."

I spend the morning doing the ranch chores in the barn. Kit Kat seems to watch me, as I move from stall to stall, cleaning out each one. I know a lot of senior ranch hands pass mucking out the stalls to the low man on the totem pole, but I don't mind it. It's an easy job that allows me to think. So, I always take a shift, when I have something on my mind.

Today, all I can think about is Lilly. She's good at what she does, there's no doubt about it. When she isn't here, I find myself missing her, and that's a dangerous road to go down.

As I finish with the stalls, the other guys and I start pulling the entire Christmas decor out of storage and sorting it out. We have it pretty much down to a routine, because the decorations are the same every year.

I'm testing out the lights when the girls come storming out of the house in their jeans, boots, and jackets. My eyes find Lilly instantly, and a huge smile lights up her face when she enters the barn. My knees feel weak when her eyes meet mine head on, but I'm pulled away by Blaze.

"Hey, ladies. Riley napping?" Blaze asks.

"Yes, and she's going to be so pissed that you didn't let her come sit out here to watch," Sage rolls her eyes.

"Then let's move fast," Blaze tries to joke, but purses his lips deep in thought.

"First, we need to make sure all the lights are working," Mac jumps in.

Everyone spreads out. Lilly, Jason, and Ella end up at the table with me, as we start untangling and testing lights.

"Ella, you should tell Mike about the phone call you had at lunch," Lilly tilts her head towards me.

"Oh! My parents decided to move to Rock Springs. Maggie and Royce jumped at the idea, and they have someone to rent their house back in Tennessee. Sage is letting them stay at one of the cabins here on the ranch, so they're going to be here just in time to spend Thanksgiving with us!"

Ella bounces on the balls of her feet, and her smile is as bright as her eyes. I know her brother Royce has been trying to get Anna Mae to look his way for a while now. Her sister Maggie seemed to fit right in the last time she was here, too.

It only takes us about twenty minutes to get the lights done, and then we break into teams. Lilly and I are on the large barn wall. Every year we take evergreen garland strung with lights and make a zig-zag Christmas tree on the side of the barn with a large, lighted star on top.

I've got the process pretty much down to a science since the nails stay in the barn all year round. Lilly and I make a great team and get it done faster than I have in the past. Once the lights are up, we both step back to take a look.

"I love how during the day the red barn and the green garland stand out, and at night, you get the lights," Lilly gushes. Her eyes sparkle, as she takes in the side of the barn, and her smile is infectious. You can't be around Lilly, when she lights up like this and not be smiling, too.

"Let's head in and see what else they need help with," I suggest.

We find Blaze who has taken over what Riley would be doing, which was organizing everyone.

"Hey, you two done with the side of the barn?" He asks when he sees us.

"Yep, what's next?" I ask him.

"Well Sage, Colt, Mac, and Sarah did the lights on the fence. Jason and Ella went to help Mom and Dad, and the ranch hands are on their side of the ranch. I hung up the wreaths on the gates. So, y'all want to do the front porch or in the barn here? I'm about to grab the guys and start stringing lights on the house."

"The barn!" Lilly claps her hands together. I can tell she's really getting into all this.

"Okay, each of the stables gets some of the decor on the gates. It doesn't matter what goes where. There's a box there for the office, too."

Blaze nods and heads out with lights for the house. We get to work decorating each gate. I love watching her decide which decoration goes where. She gave each stall its own theme. Some include horseshoes, some have ropes, some have wreaths, there's a set of cowboy boots with poinsettias in them, a wagon wheel wreath, and several Texas stars.

I'm hanging some lights around the barn when I hear Lilly.

"What do you think, Kit Kat? Do you want horseshoes or Christmas trees for your stall, huh?"

I look over, seeing her holding up two decorations in front of the horse, and when Kit Kat leans forward and touches her nose to the Christmas tree, Lilly laughs, and it fills the whole barn.

"Christmas trees it is." She sets the items down and gets to work on the stall. I find myself glancing her way every few minutes, watching her work, and Kit Kat can't take her eyes off Lilly either.

When we are finished with the barn, we go decorate the office.

"We don't normally do too much in here, but Sage insists it gets decorated, too," I tell her.

We set up the small tabletop tree that has lights already attached and place a few ornaments on it. I string some lights around the windows, and Lilly hangs some wreaths on the walls.

Her pine and cherry scent fill the room, and while we work in silence, I'm very aware of where she is in the room. I finish up the last window and turn to find Lilly, hanging the last wreath.

"There, now the barn is Christmas ready," Lilly turns and smiles at me. She doesn't realize how close I am when she turns, so I reach out and grip her hips to stop her from running into me, making her smile falter. That draws my attention right to her lips that part slightly.

I'm not thinking clearly, because having Lilly in my arms and so close to me, feels perfect. It feels right like she belongs here.

I don't remove my eyes from her lips, as I lean in slowly. When her tongue darts out and licks her lips, I know she's feeling this pull, too. I lean in, until I'm centimeters from her lips, and I can feel her warm breath mix with mine.

"Hey, this barn looks amazing!" Ella comes bouncing in the office, and Lilly and I shoot apart, like repelled magnets. There's a blush coating Lilly's cheeks, and it takes me a minute to regain my thoughts.

"Well, it was all Lilly's doing. She's great with decorating," I tell Ella.

I hear a ping, and Lilly pulls out her phone.

"Ahhh, Riley is up, and I'm being summoned. Tell Blaze he should probably finish. I'm sure we're about to get hell for this."

Ella laughs, "I'll go in with you and get hot chocolate going for everyone."

She loops her arm in Lilly's, and all I can do is stare and watch them head for the house.

What the hell just happened?

Chapter 7

Lilly

Mike's parents are the typical supportive parents. They love him, and that's obvious by how much they try to fit in, which only makes them stand out more, around here anyway.

They did some shopping in Dallas and picked up what they are calling their cowboy attire. They are in jeans, flannel shirts, boots, and cowboy hats. It's all new, and you can tell they are not the jean wearing type.

As I stand off to the side, I watch them show their support. His mom looks at the other women and tries to imitate what they do, and his dad does the same. He picked up the hat tipping part pretty quickly.

"It's some sight, isn't it?" Sage says, coming to stand beside me.

"Yeah, I'm trying not to laugh, because they're being supportive, but it sure is a sight to see. I wasn't that bad when I first got here, was I?"

"No way, it's one thing I liked about you. You were just a take it or leave it girl. It's a lot like the attitude I formed while traveling. Though as a tip from one girl to another, it's okay to let your guard down every now and then."

The smell of the Thanksgiving meal starts to fill the event barn, and Sage smiles. "Guess that's my cue to get back to work."

This is the first Thanksgiving I've been at the ranch, and just like Texas is known for, it's a go big or go home state of mind. They set up one long table in the event barn that can easily hold over fifty people. They have all the hands who are spending the holiday on the ranch, included in the meal.

There's a corner for kids with games, crafts, and a drawing table. Their place setting is more fun, and even some of the adults are over there, joining them in the games. Most of the kids are those of the ranch hands, and next year, it will include Riley and Megan's little ones.

"Okay, everyone." Colt stands, getting everyone's attention. "My wife," he pauses for a brief moment and smiles, "has told me to get you all seated. There are place cards because she wanted to make sure everyone got to mingle. So, find your seats, as we finish up."

Some people had already scouted out their seats and made a beeline there. I slowly walk around the table, until I find my place card, right next to Mike's. I also recognize Riley's handwriting on them. I shake my head, as Mike walks up and pulls my seat out.

"Looks like you're stuck with me, firecracker." His warm breath dances across my ear, but I say nothing, as I take my seat.

Mike's parents are sitting across from us. They make it a point to introduce themselves to everyone near them, before getting in line for the buffet-style meal.

I guess, the kitchen at both the main houses, along with the ones here at the event barn, had been going for days. I made over ten apple pies myself, but then I was banned from biscuit duty because I was doing it wrong. I was also banned from bacon duty because I was eating too much of it.

I think they took mercy on me when Mike popped in and asked me to come help with the setup. Sitting here now and taking it all in, everyone talking and laughing, and kids running back and forth, I realize this is the home I have been looking for. I had a much smaller version of this growing up, but as we got older, we all went off to do our own things, as it should be.

Like me, Mike's parents have also tried a little bit of everything at the buffet table. I will say Thanksgiving here is like nothing I have ever seen.

I lean over and whisper to Mike, "Do they get to go home for Thanksgiving to visit family?" I nod towards the ranch hands.

"There's an A/B rotation. When you get hired, you get assigned to shift A or B. Shift A could go home for Thanksgiving this year but has to stay and work Christmas. Next year, they can go home for Christmas but have to work Thanksgiving. The chores don't stop just because it's a holiday, and this keeps it fair. Sage and Blaze encourage everyone who has to stay because they're working to invite their families to join them here. Some do for the experience."

Sage runs the west side of the ranch with her husband, Colt, and Blaze runs the east side with Mac. Their parents are pretty much retired but are still very active on the ranch. Their sister Megan owns the beauty salon, and a few of her girls are here today, too. Her husband, Hunter, is a vet like his dad, and his parents have joined us.

Jason, the oldest brother, owns the bar and restaurant in town, and his wife Ella is beaming now that her family has moved to town. Mac and Sarah put off their honeymoon just to be here for Thanksgiving and leave for the lake house tonight. So, everyone is here.

"Are we late?" An older woman walks in with a woman my age.

Megan jumps up, "Mrs. Willow! Anna Mae! No, never." Megan gives each of them a hug and directs them to the food table. Royce, Ella's brother, is instantly right there next to Anna Mae, helping her make a plate and sitting beside her at the table. Anyone could see there's something there. I can also tell Anna Mae is trying to keep him at arm's length. *Poor guy.*

I have to wonder how long that will last. Royce helps her grandma as needed, and you can tell her grandma is playing matchmaker, just like Riley, and it's fun to watch.

I'm jolted back to the people in front of me when Mike runs his hand along my arm.

"Sorry, what did I miss?" I ask.

"We were just wondering what it's like to be on the road. Do you get to see any of the places you visit?" Laura, Mike's mom, asks.

"Yes, sometimes. My last run took me to Flagstaff, and I was able to have dinner with my parents. They winter down in Sedona and then spend the warmer summer months in Montana. Sometimes, the timeline is so fast I only see the road, and sometimes, I have half a day to explore."

"What is one of your favorite routes to drive?" Will, Mike's dad, asks.

I momentarily draw a blank, as Mike's arm rubs up against me again, as he cuts the food on his plate. He smiles over at me like he knows exactly what he's doing.

Clearing my throat, I respond, "I like driving The Rockies. Most truckers hate driving in the mountains, but I like the views and the challenge. The flat road gets boring. A friend of mine started driving the ice roads in Canada and has been trying to get me up there, but I don't think I'm up for it. The pictures she sends me are amazing, though."

"Like the ice truckers show on TV?" Will asks.

"Yeah, and to be honest, I watched the show, and it's why I won't do it. I know they over exaggerate it for TV, but still. I don't have a death wish. Plus, I'm pretty sure my mom would drag me back to the lower forty-eight by my ear if I tried."

This makes everyone laugh. "Can't say I blame her." Laura agrees.

Maggie sits down on my other side with a sigh.

"Happy to be here and settled?" I ask her.

"Yes, I love it here. Don't get me wrong, it's just..." She pauses like she's trying to figure out how to word things. "We are no longer with the church in Tennessee, and I don't want to follow their rules."

"Like what?" I ask. I know they had a more conservative upbringing, because of the church their parents worked at.

"Well, I want to wear jeans. I think jeans are modest, right? It's just not practical to wear dresses and skirts around the ranch."

"Yes, jeans are modest, and it all depends on the shirts you pair them with. They're almost a must if you plan to ride horses on a regular basis. Have you talked to your parents?" I ask her.

"No, I'm going to wait, until after everyone is more settled."

Maggie and I talk more about her plans while here. She hints around about a possible guy but doesn't give me much to go on. I think she and I are going to be friends. She's easygoing and has a good head on her shoulders.

We both get pulled into a conversation about the ranch decorations. Mike is never far from my side, and it feels natural like this is where I was always meant to be.

I catch Riley looking over at me a few times and smiling. Once she even winked, letting me know that she knows she was caught. There's something in her smile that's a bit mischievous, and it makes me wonder what is up her sleeve.

That night lying in bed I think about the last few days, and how much I have felt at home here, and then start to wonder, if Rock Springs is where I'm meant to be.

Chapter 8

Mike

I'm lying in bed, fighting against having to open my eyes, when there's a knock on my door. I grunt, grumble, and then get out of bed to open the door. I didn't expect to find Lilly on the other side, and her eyes go big, as they crawl down my body.

I look down, realizing I'm shirtless and in gray sweatpants. This is the most I sleep in, as the weather turns cold. I didn't think twice about answering the door like this.

I chuckle at her reaction, as I lean against the door frame and cross my arms. I will admit I like being able to throw Lilly off kilter, and knowing I can affect her this way, gives me pleasure.

I return the favor and let my eyes roam over her. Her jeans look like they were painted on, and her red and green flannel is festive for the upcoming Christmas season. Her brown cowgirl boots have red stitching to match the shirt, and her hair is pulled over her shoulder in a loose braid.

She holds up a piece of paper.

"Riley is insisting I go do her Christmas shopping today since it's Black Friday. She wants me to go into Dallas, and Blaze is insisting you drive me since there's bad weather coming. Not like I don't drive for a living or anything. She also apparently made Mac and Sarah leave early to get to the lake house for their honeymoon before it hit."

I laugh, as she rolls her eyes at that before she continues. "I guess your parents are spending the day with Blaze on the ranch. They want to learn the ropes, I think."

That sounds like them. Though, I wish they had been here a few years ago, instead of waiting until now. I can't be too mad. I'm just happy they are here.

I open the door wider, "Come in, while I get ready."

I stay in a small cabin next to the bunkhouse. It's nothing special with only two rooms. One is the living room and kitchen with a bar area for a table, and the other is the bedroom with a small bathroom. It's more than enough for me, and it's also one of the perks of getting promoted to senior ranch hand when I got to get out of the bunkhouse and have my own space.

I'm ready to go in record time with the thought of spending the day with Lilly motivating me. As I'm walking to my truck, she stops me.

"Where are you going?" She calls after me.

"To my truck," I point to it.

"Why do you get to drive?" I sigh and run my hands through my hair.

"You said bad weather is coming, and my truck is ready for any kind of Texas weather. Besides, around here, it's the gentlemanly thing to do to drive and fight traffic, so you can relax and think about shopping." I open the truck door for her.

She doesn't even hide that she rolls her eyes, as she gets in the truck. She's quiet, as we head out of town. I stop at the Dairy Queen, the only thing close to fast food around here, and I order breakfast and coffee for us.

We eat in silence until we hit the highway.

"So, what's on this list?" I ask her.

Lilly pulls the list out and starts reading.

"She even marked what order we're to hit the stores. First, is the baby boutique she's been talking about. I guess, she called in an order, so we just have to pick it up, thankfully. Then, we're to hit the western store to pick up some gifts for the guys. Then, Target for some home decor and baby things, and then a few stores she has orders for us to get. After that, we're to stop at two bakeries. One to get five pounds of peppermint bark, and another to get five dozen donuts. I think she's messing with us."

"Nope, the donuts and peppermint bark are a tradition. You can't come into Dallas, during the holidays and head home without them unless you want a ranch full of angry people. Trust me, I forgot once, and no one would talk to me for a week. I ended up making a special trip back just to get them."

As I watch the miles of country land slowly get more and more populated, I'm wracking my brain for a Christmas gift for Lilly. Ever since our almost kiss that day decorating the barn, she has been on my mind constantly.

I won't admit it to her, but I'm thrilled to have been pushed on this little shopping trip to have more time with her. I'm like a moth drawn to a flame. She draws me in and holds my attention, even when I'm not aware of it.

Our first stop, we are in and out, but our second stop at the western store takes a bit longer to find everything on Riley's list. I wander off at one point, picking up some items for gifts. Then, I see something that would be perfect for Lilly, and I make sure she isn't around.

It's a horseshoe decorated in turquoise and silver with a plaque in the center. It's the perfect size to put the ranch's brand on it. I bury it with a few of my other purchases and check out, just before she places her stuff on the counter.

"Find everything?" I ask her.

"Yep. I swear next Christmas, I'm making her do my shopping for me. It's only fair," Lilly huffs.

"Why? You plan to be knocked up and on bed rest?" As soon as I say it, I can't help but picture Lilly pregnant. Her belly round and her breasts overflowing from her top, while being able to put my hand on her and feeling our baby kick.

Whoa, my dick is getting harder by the second at the thought of Lilly pregnant with my baby, and I need to calm down the thoughts. It doesn't stop my heart from racing, or my palms from sweating, though.

This is exactly the distraction I don't need, I remind myself. Once I find a ranch, it's going to take a good year to get it up and going, and there's no time for babies or even a wife.

"No, maybe just a twisted ankle on Thanksgiving will work." Lilly laughs, and I feel it in my cock. This girl does something to me, and the more I'm around her, the stronger the pull is, and the more time I want with her.

After a few more stops, my stomach starts rumbling.

"Hey, want to grab lunch? I know a great little sub shop a few blocks down." I ask her.

"Sure, I could use a bit of a break. Can we walk there?"

I nod and lead the way. We are in downtown Dallas, and the stores lining the streets all have their Christmas lights and decorations up, along with huge sales signs in the window, advertising Black Friday sales.

There isn't much of a crowd at the sub shop, so we are able to get our food and a table.

"How did you find this place?" She asks.

"By pure accident, one of the first times I was in town. They had the door open, and a special on meatballs subs. The smell drew me in. I've stopped here pretty much every time since. Have you heard from your sister?"

Just like that, she launches off into the details of the tour. She talks about her sister recording the album, and even trying to meet up on one of her tour dates.

I make a mental note that if I ever need to get her talking to ask about her family. She can go on and on about them, but she's hesitant to talk about herself.

After lunch, we finish up shopping and then go to the bakery.

"Wow," Lilly says, as we step inside.

I agree with that statement. The bakery is bright white with fake snow everywhere, and all the décor is red. Large, shiny, red ornaments are hanging from the ceiling, and even red lights are strung all around the counter.

"Last year, they did the place up in blue and silver," I mumble, as I take everything in.

"Dallas Cowboys' colors." Lilly laughs. "Alright, show me these things we can't come home without."

This year the shop with the donuts is also making peppermint bark. After a little taste testing, we grab the peppermint bark and donuts and make our way home. Laughing, we wonder if anyone will notice they aren't from the second bakery.

We made a great team today, and I enjoyed her company. As she texts her sister, my mind wanders to how good a team we might be on the ranch, too.

Chapter 9

Mike

"Son, did you hear me?"

"Sorry, Dad," I shake my head, trying to clear away the thoughts of shopping yesterday with Lilly.

I have never had so much fun shopping, as I did with her. We laughed so hard at things people were buying. She let me buy her lunch, and as far as I'm concerned, it was a date. We talked about Christmas's growing up, and I even made her a believer of the peppermint bark and donuts. So much so, she bought extras.

Today, I'm looking at the two ranches my dad found. We pulled up to the first one, and I missed what my dad said.

"What's on your mind, baby?" Mom loops her arm through mine.

"Lilly," I see no point in beating around the bush with my parents.

"I like her. She's strong and will keep you on your toes," Mom nods.

I smile, and to keep Mom from going down the matchmaking trail, I turn to my dad, "So, tell me about this ranch."

It's about thirty minutes outside Rock Springs, so location wise, it's good, but it's a bit more than I was looking to spend. It's also one hundred acres more than I was looking at.

The house in front of me doesn't look too bad. It has a stone front and a wraparound porch. It's set up on a hill higher than the rest of the property, so you know it has beautiful views.

"Well, this house needs some work, but there's already a bunkhouse on the property and a stable. I was told the stable was set up to be expanded later. There's a creek at the back of the property. It's also set up for hunting, which would make some good options when the summer camp is closed. The current owners will knock the price down if we don't want the cattle, which I'm assuming you don't."

"No, Dad. I have no plans for cattle, but with the additional acreage, it could be an extra income. I'd have to weigh the costs."

He nods, "I was thinking the same thing. There's a personal garden behind the home already plowed and ready to go as well. Oh, here's Ryan."

Ryan turns out to be the realtor my dad has been talking to. He looks to be my age, and his boots are heavily worn. The sign for a true Texan and not someone putting on an act.

We view the ranch house first, and Dad's right, it does needs work. The wood floors need to be redone, and the kitchen looks like it hasn't been touched, since the 50's. There's a show stopping fireplace in the living room made from the same rocks that are on the outside of the house. There are some great views of the property from the house as well.

"Does everything work?" I point to the kitchen.

"Oh yes, and if you make an offer, I will get an inspector out here to make sure of it," Ryan says in his Texan drawl. I snap a few photos, before moving to look at the bedrooms. There are three bedrooms on one side of the house that look like they have been used as kids' rooms, and the master is at the other end. I just can't see myself living here, but I head out to check out the rest of the ranch.

We spend a few hours being given a tour on the Gator they used to get around the ranch and seeing all the ranch has to offer. Ryan also had a few overhead aerial videos he showed us, too.

"So, what did you think?" Ryan asks my dad, and my dad smiles.

"Well, you need to ask Mike. He's buying, and I just set up the tours." I don't miss the hint of pride in my dad's eyes.

Ryan's eyes turn on me, "It's more land than I need, and to be honest, it's just not a fit. The stable is too small, and at this price, there wouldn't be any money left to add on to it. The creek is nice, but there's no place to set up and enjoy it."

We talk about a few other things, and we head off to the second place for sale.

I like the front gate set up and begin to hope this property might be the one. There's a huge spring-fed lake that's stocked for fishing that we pass on our way to the main house.

This place is nice, and I could see a family living there, just not my family. The barn needs too much work for it to be ready-to-use right away.

Ryan says he's going to take my notes and send me some links for other possible places.

When I get back to the ranch later that day, I walk in, and it looks like the North Pole exploded in the main house.

"What's all this?" I ask.

"Well, Riley went overboard, since she can't be up decorating," Megan tilts her head towards the couch, where Riley sits with her feet up.

I take in the lights framing every window, and the garland framing every doorway. There are large Christmas signs on the wall, and the regular blankets and pillows have all been replaced with Christmas ones. The formal dining room table is set with red and silver Christmas settings.

"You're missing a tree," I point out.

"Soon enough!" Riley laughs. "Mike, will you help Lilly with the fireplace? Those lanterns need to go up there, and the stockings need to be hung."

That's when I notice Lily over by the fireplace. The light from the fire dancing across her face brings out the honey color in her hair, and I've never seen her look more beautiful.

"What are you going to do, when you all have kids? There won't be enough room for more stockings," I joke, trying to lighten the mood.

"Hang them on the wall," Riley shrugs.

Lilly and I both laugh and start setting up the lanterns on the mantle. The stocking hangers get put up, and we start debating on what order to put the stockings.

When I turn to get Riley's approval, I see her looking at Lilly with an odd look on her face, and her head tilted to the side. When she sees me glancing at her, the look is gone, and she offers me one of the smiles she's known for.

I know that look, and it means trouble. The last time I saw it was when she tried to play matchmaker with Sarah and Mac.

Chapter 10

Lilly

I'm sitting around the table with the family eating breakfast when Mike walks in.

"Hey, Blaze. I just got a call from Chuck, the foreman of the land that butts up to us on the north side. He said one of our bulls is caught in the fence by the creek. He's shorthanded and doesn't have anyone to get it free. He gave the bull a sedative to calm him, but we need to get out there."

"Shit, we have a doctor's appointment today," He looks at Riley, and she looks at me.

"Lilly will go help. Please? You'll pass the area where the Christmas trees are, and you know what I want for the house. You can get one on your way back. And get some of those pinecones we were talking about. Please?"

I look at Mike, "Can we do it just the two of us?"

"Yeah, but we got to go now because I have the truck loaded with the Gator," he says, tilting his head towards the door.

I jump up and grab my jacket, as we head out. We drive as far as we can on the ranch road, before getting off and hopping in the Gator the rest of the way. I can tell he's concentrating on the task at hand, but I feel a need to break the silence.

"Did your parents make it home okay?" I ask.

"Yeah, they're already making plans to come back. Dad is talking like he and Ryan, the real estate agent, are best friends now."

When we get to the tree clearing, I'm not sure what to expect, but the massive bull lying on the ground isn't it. I know cows are big, but it's now I realize I'm not sure I've ever seen a bull on the ranch because this guy is huge.

He almost looks like a small truck on the ground. He is pure muscle with horns long enough to do some serious damage.

"Hey, Chuck. This is Lilly. Thanks for staying with him," Mike says.

The cowboy leaning on the fence tilts his hat in a hello, as I quickly take him in. There has to be something in the water around here with all the good looking cowboys.

It should be illegal.

Chuck looks like one of those rough cowboys that just stepped out of the TV, even though he's not as handsome as Mike.

"No problem, and he isn't badly injured. I thought he'd be a lot worse. It looks like he was trying to stick his head through to eat the grass, and then started thrashing around, because of the wire around his neck."

"He's lucky it's not one of the electric wires. How much longer will he be out?"

"Half an hour at most."

"Okay, let's cut this wire and get it off him. We need to get some antibiotics in him before he wakes." Mike starts giving orders, and Chuck helps, as he cuts the wire fence and gets it off the bull. He attaches a second ear tag, as the huge animal stirs.

"What's that for?" I ask because it doesn't have a number or anything on it, like the other one.

"It's a GPS tag, so we can find him later and have Hunter take a look at him. There's no way we can get him back to the barn before this weather hits," he points over my shoulder at the clouds rolling in.

Looking behind me, I see the dark clouds against the otherwise bright sky. It looks like they are chasing after us.

Mike quickly gives the bull a shot, of what I assume is antibiotics, and then pulls me away from the animal, as he starts to move his head and get his bearings. Mike stands in front of me, and I have to peek around his shoulder to watch the animal slowly get up and stagger to his feet.

If I didn't know any better, I'd say the bull was drunk. He looks at the fence then turns our way, and I place a hand on Mike's back. I can feel how tense he is. He reaches his hand back and pulls me completely behind him. A moment later, I see the animal walking off towards the tree line away from the fence. It's only then that Mike starts to relax.

"You two okay with the fence? I'm going to try to beat this storm back to the barn. We're too short handed for me to be stuck out here," Chuck says.

"Yeah, we got this. Go and let us know what we owe you for the sedative," Mike says, as he shakes his hand.

Chuck mounts his horse and then looks back at us. "Nothing but a favor to be called in if needed down the road."

"Anytime, you've got my number. If you guys need help, let me know. We can spare a guy or two after Christmas." With another round of thanks, Chuck tips his hat to me and rides off.

"Come on, Lilly. Let's get this fence fixed, and then we can make it to one of the cabins. I don't think we'll make it back to the truck," Mike says, as he hands me a pair of gloves.

Watching him work and stretch the fence is a sight to see. There's a reason cowboys have the muscles they do, and it's because of work like this. They aren't like the gym muscles that are perfectly sculpted. No, these are the hard earned muscles of hard work day in and day out, and they are much sexier.

He explains what he's doing and why to me, as he goes, and I try to pay attention, as I hold part of the fence or hand him tools. But I'm mesmerized watching him work. He's so sure in what he's doing, and his movements are that of someone who's done them a hundred times.

Once the fence is fixed, we pack the Gator and go a slightly different way than before.

There are many cabins on the ranch to ride out bad weather in. There's a little area for the Gator to park, or even to shelter horses if needed. Mike secures everything before we head inside. No sooner does the door close, then the rain starts pouring down, causing us both to laugh.

"Okay, let's get a fire going," Mike grabs some wood from beside the wood stove in the corner, and the cabin slowly starts to warm.

I sit on the couch and watch him work. I realize it's quickly becoming one of my favorite things to do.

"They're calling for snow in a few days. Dave called me and told me if it snows my route will be canceled, so I might have another week's vacation," I tell him.

He finishes with the stove and turns to look at me.

"Well, I'm glad you won't be driving in the snow," he says.

"I've driven in the snow before, but I'd rather not."

He sits down next to me, pulling a blanket off the back of the couch, and then covers us both up. "It's going to take a few minutes for the cabin to warm up."

"So, I didn't know they grew Christmas trees on the ranch," I ask.

"They aren't your typical pine trees. They're a Ponderous Pine, and they have to be cut into the shape of a traditional Christmas tree. But it's a Texas tree for a Texas Christmas," Mike laughs, and he wraps his arm around my shoulder, pulling me in. I rest my head on his shoulder and sigh, soaking in his warmth.

"Are you warm enough?" He asks, his voice laced with concern.

I lift my head and look up at him. "Yeah, it's starting to warm up."

His eyes meet mine, and I'm suddenly aware that I'm pressed up against him, and there are only a few inches separating my lips from his. It's almost like he realizes it too, as he draws in a sharp intake of breath, but neither of us moves. I can feel myself growing wetter, as my bra stretches across my stiff nipples.

His hand comes up and tangles in my hair, and then his mouth crashes down on mine. This kiss isn't like any other kiss I've ever had in my life. It's consuming, and I can't get enough, but I want it to slow down at the same time.

I sit up and lean into the kiss, as I bunch my hand against the fabric of his shirt to pull him closer. His teeth drag lightly over my lower lip, making me gasp, while he deepens the kiss. His tongue slides against mine, making love to my mouth, the way I wish another part of him was making love to another part of me.

He guides me down on my back and props himself up over me, all the while, not breaking the kiss. I reach for his shirt, but he takes my hands in his, holding them above my head.

"Do you know how long I've been waiting to kiss you?" He asks, as his lips travel down my neck.

"How long?" I ask breathlessly, tilting my head back and encouraging him on.

"Seven months, since Sage and Colt's wedding."

I moan his name, as he slides his teeth over the pulse point on my neck before he starts kissing his way back up to my mouth. He claims me with this kiss, dominating me and demanding my surrender to it. I give it to him because it feels so good to let go in that moment.

He grinds into me, and I feel how hard he is. I lift my hips to meet his and get my hands free to undo his shirt.

He takes my hand in his again and pulls back to look at me.

"This isn't going to go any further, firecracker. I want it to, believe me," he says, rolling his hips into mine to prove his point.

"But I haven't even taken you out on an actual date."

"We had lunch in Dallas, and that was the best date I've had in years," I tell him.

"I didn't get a kiss at the end, so it wasn't a date." He runs his nose along my neck.

"Then this is just a delayed end of date kiss," I whisper.

He pulls back, sits up, and takes me up with him. "Come here, let me hold you, and we can talk, while we're waiting out the storm."

We chat about the properties he saw with his dad, and what he's looking for in a ranch. We talk about the storm they say is coming and about the bull from this morning. We talk so long that I didn't notice the sun go down, until both our stomachs rumble.

He smiles, rubbing his nose against mine. "Let me feed you. Then, I guess we should plan to stay here for the night since it's still raining pretty good out there."

I nod, and we make our way into the kitchen. "So, we have canned chili and some beef jerky," Mike looks at me.

"Sounds perfect."

He pulls out a pot and gets the chili warmed up on the woodstove, while I set the table. I find a brand new case of bottled water for us, and then give the dishes and silverware a quick wash and dry, before putting them on the table.

It doesn't escape me how easy he is to talk to, while we eat and pass the time, as the rain holds us hostage inside.

Chapter 11

Mike

Holy hell, that was the best night's sleep I can remember having in a long time. Then, I feel a warm body shift against me, and my eyes pop open.

Lilly.

It all comes rushing back to me. We stayed up late talking and kissing, and I fell asleep with her in my arms.

She's still sleeping with her back pressed to my front, so I enjoy the feel of her against me, the warmth of her skin, as I take in her soft, brown hair scattered across the pillow, and her lips slightly swollen from all the kissing. I want to puff my chest out, when I see those lips, knowing they are swollen, because of me.

Not being able to stop myself, I run my nose down her neck, taking in her elusive pine and cherry scent. As I start kissing up her neck from her shoulder, she stirs, and I keep kissing until she moans and turns her head to look at me.

"How am I going to sleep alone now that I know what it's like to hold you in my arms all night?" I ask her.

She doesn't answer me. She just turns her head and kisses me. A kiss I try to deepen, but she pulls away with a smile on her face.

"That was one hell of a first date, cowboy," she smiles.

"That was not a first date."

"Yes, it was. You cooked for me, we spent a lot of time talking, and you kissed me."

I open my mouth but then close it again. She's right, it was everything I said our first date needed to be. It was easy and fun, and the best first date of my life.

"Fine, our second date starts now. Let's get ready and go pick out this Christmas tree."

Once ready and done securing the cabin, we grab some jerky for breakfast and head out to find the ground covered in ice.

"Well, I didn't plan for that," I mutter. I'm thankful the Gator is all terrain, and that includes ice and snow, even if I have to drive a bit slower back to the truck. We load up the truck, thankful for the heat, as we get going.

It's not a far drive to the patch with the trees we cut for Christmas, but we are going slowly thanks to the ice. At our destination, we get out and walk along the trees, as Lilly takes in each one.

"So, once back at the house, the tree gets cut into shape?" She asks, staring at the giant blob of a tree.

"Yeah, but trust me, they look really nice."

"Okay then, this one should work; it's tall enough for what Riley wants. It's full, so it'll trim up nice, right?"

I give the tree a good once over, "Yes it will, but we don't need one this tall."

"Yes, we do. Riley said she wanted one taller than Blaze. He's taller than you, so this is the tree."

"Why does she need one so tall?"

"Because she's pregnant, miserable, and it's what she wants." Lilly huffs at me, and I finally give in. Can't upset the pregnant lady, or there will be hell to pay.

As I cut the tree down, Lilly works on getting the pinecones Riley wants for decorations, and then helps get the tree to the truck. It takes twice as long to get back to the main house, because of the ice, and about halfway there, it starts to lightly snow. By the time we pull up to the barn, the snow has picked up, and there's already a good inch of it on the ground.

"I think this is going to be worse than they said," I shake my head, looking out over the pasture.

"Why?" She asks.

"Well at most, we get maybe three inches of snow each year, and it's supposed to snow for a few days, and it's already piling up fast."

We get the tree inside, and Lilly heads up to check on Riley, while the guys help me set the tree up in the barn and trim it.

"Where were you two last night?" Blaze asks.

"Took a little bit longer with the bull. Chuck had him knocked out when we got there. He looks good though, and I got a tracker on him. Hunter will need to check on him, as soon as he can. I also gave him a dose of the antibiotic. Once he was up, we fixed the fence and barely made it to the cabin, before the rain hit. When we woke up, it was all ice. Took twice as long to get back here. There's already an inch of snow on the ground out there."

"Shit," Colt says.

"Hey, we closed WJ's. They're calling for close to a foot of snow," Jason comes in and joins us.

WJ's is the bar he and Ella turned into a family restaurant in town. Nick works there and just won a BBQ Championship in Dallas, so the place has been featured in the state quite a bit.

"We haven't had snow like that in over ten years," Blaze whistles.

"The ranch ready for that?" I ask them.

"As ready as we can be," Blaze nods.

• • • ● • ● • • •

That night I'm in bed, going over a list of things to check on in the morning. I spent the rest of the day securing what I could, but at this point, we are in a wait and see mode.

When I hear a knock at my door, I worry I missed something. Opening the door, I find Lilly on my doorstep, and a different sensation takes over my body. I grow hard at just the sight of her. She pushes her way in, and I close and lock the door.

"So, turns out I can't sleep now either. Then, I was thinking that the first night a couple sleeps in the same bed usually involves an orgasm, so I totally got gypped here."

My mind is blank, so my body takes over, and before I know it, I have her in my arms, and my lips are on hers. My hand cradles the back of the head, tilting her so I can fully taste her lips. Her arms wrap around my neck and pull me closer, as I walk us back towards my bed.

Her hands trail down my naked chest, and the feel of her skin on my skin sends shock waves, causing my cock to harden between us.

I slip her jacket off and find her in a thin tank top, no bra, and flannel pants.

"This what you sleep in?" I ask as I take her in. Her full, round breasts, and the hourglass nip of her waist with hips perfect for grabbing and holding, while she rides me.

She shrugs, "More or less."

"Get in the bed, firecracker."

She smiles at me, climbs on to the bed, and then lies down. I start pulling her pants off, but an uncertain look crosses her face.

"What are you doing?" She asks.

"You wanted to cum, so you'll cum on my face." She bites her lip, so I let go of her pants and move to lie beside her.

"If you don't want this, just say so. I'm not going to do anything you don't want. I'm perfectly okay to lay here with you in my arms, too."

"It's just well... no one has...." She sighs, "Put their face down there before."

I groan. "I want to, Lilly. I want to taste you and make you cum on my tongue, but not until you're ready."

She takes a deep breath, and a moment later, she nods. "I'm ready."

"You sure?"

"Mike, I want you so bad it hurts. Yes, I'm sure."

"Can't have my girl hurting, now can we?" I murmur, as I plant a kiss on top of each breast over her tank top, before moving down and slowly taking off her pants and underwear.

When she's bare to me from the waist down, I can't help but stare.

"God, Lilly, you're so damn beautiful."

I settle between her thighs, spreading them wide, and get my first taste of her when I lick her from slit to clit. She tastes like that cinnamon lip gloss she wears all the time. I swear I'm addicted to her. When I run my tongue on her clit, her hips buck. I use one hand to hold her still, and then slide a finger into her.

She's so tight and warm, and as I try to add a second finger, she clamps down on me. I slow down, changing up my pace, and she lets out a frustrated squeal.

I stretch her slowly, and then pick up my pace. Her hands tug at my hair, as she pulls me closer, and her thighs lock around my head. She cums with my name on her lips, and I swallow every drop she gives me until she's relaxed and limp. I kiss my way up her belly, moving her shirt until I get to her breasts.

When I get my first view of them, they take my breath away. Round with dark pink nipples that are pebbled, because of me. I suck one into my mouth, flicking my tongue over it, and then do the same to the other, before covering them again and kissing up her neck.

When my lips finally land on hers, my moan is involuntary. I almost lose it, when her hand lands on my cock, which is leaking come into my boxer briefs.

"Not tonight, Lilly," I mumble against her lips.

"How is it fair that you got to see me cum, but I don't get to see you?"

"I'm barely holding it here together, Lilly."

"All the more reason for me to help you find release. Please, Mike." She begs, and I know now I will never be able to tell her no when she begs like that.

"Oh, God." I roll on to my back, and she starts kissing down my chest. I try to think of gross cattle births, as she takes my cock out. Just her hands on me have me ready to spill.

I open my eyes just in time to watch her lips slide down my shaft, and I grip the sheets to regain some control.

"Fuck, I'm not going to last long. I'd be embarrassed if I didn't just have my head between your thighs."

Even from here, I can see the flush cover her cheeks, and it's so sexy. Her warm, wet mouth covers my cock, as she runs her tongue up the underside with each stroke.

When she swirls her tongue around the head of my cock, the tingling down my spine starts pulling at my lower back. When she cups my balls, I don't even get a warning, as I start cumming harder than I have ever cum in my life. I roar her name, as she swallows every drop.

When I'm spent, she kisses her way back up my chest, before I pull her in to lie on top of me.

She tries to move to the side, but I just tighten my hold. "Don't move," I mumble.

"I don't want to crush you."

I chuckle, "You aren't that heavy, firecracker. Now, stop moving."

I pull the blanket over us and rub her back until she falls asleep. I'm starting to drift off when I have the scariest thought I have had in a long time.

A conversation my parents had with me a while back floats to my mind. They told me to focus on my goals and limit distractions. Then, my dad reminded me of how he met my mom. She was a distraction he kept trying to avoid, but my mom stepped in, saying there are some distractions you just can't live without.

Commitment to Lilly might be a distraction I can't live without.

Chapter 12
Lilly

It snowed for three days, and it just stopped last night. Everyone was getting a bit stir crazy, so I think the break is welcome, even if it means fighting the fallen snow to check on the ranch.

We have done just about everything snow related to keep busy, including making snow ice cream, snowmen, and snow angels. Mac and Sarah are coming home today, even though they were told to stay until the snow cleared. They wanted to be around to help. Sarah also wanted to see the ranch covered in snow. So, Riley has made us wait to decorate the Christmas tree until they are here.

Every night, I have been sneaking out to Mike's cabin and then spending the night with him. It hasn't gone any further, but it's still mind-blowing every night.

We haven't told anyone about us, but then again, we haven't talked about where we stand. For all I know, I'm just someone to warm his bed, because I know he doesn't want anything to distract him from his ranch, and a relationship would be a huge distraction.

I have convinced myself I'm okay with that since as soon as the roads are cleared, I will be back on the road. I have seen time and time again that relationships don't work with me, while I'm on the road, so I have just stopped trying.

I'm helping make lunch, when I get a call from my boss, Dave.

"Hey, Dave."

"Hey, Lilly. The weather report near you says you're going to get a few more inches of snow tonight. Being as far out as you are, it'll be a few days, before the roads are plowed enough for me to send you to Dallas. I guess you'll be down another week."

"Damn."

"Yeah, but I'll be in touch in a few days. Don't do anything stupid. Wait for the roads to be cleared and salted, before driving that rig."

"Okay, I promise, Dave."

"Stay safe, Lilly."

After lunch, Sarah and Mac get home, and we start on the tree. Blaze has Riley propped up on the couch, and she has mastered giving orders to design the perfect tree.

"So Mom, last night Riley was bugging me about a change of scenery. Please, tell me you haven't canceled the ranch Christmas party at your house tonight?" Blaze begs.

"No, dear. I haven't, but I don't know who all will show up in this weather."

"Well, we'll all be there," Sage says, and we all agree.

"It's not too bad to get the ranch hands there. We'll make sure the driveway is cleared enough, and I'll offer rides to anyone who needs them," Colt adds.

"Then I better get home and get the food going!" Helen laughs, before saying her goodbyes.

• • • • • • • • • •

I'm getting ready to head over to Tim and Helen's house on the other side of the ranch for the Christmas party when Mike walks into the kitchen, where I'm putting on my boots.

"Damn, look at you, sexy," he says, pulling me in for a kiss.

"Stop, anyone could walk in," I try to push him away.

"So, let them see."

I stop struggling. "You want people to know about us?"

That can't be right, there's too much at stake for him to want anything serious with me.

"Hell yes, I do." Then his posture goes stiff. "What do you think is going on here, Lilly?"

I let the words sink in, trying to understand them. Why would he want people to know about us? He knows I'm getting back on the road, so how does he think that will work? Even if I settle here in Rock Springs, being on the road, will eventually be too much to handle for him, so I decide to go with the truth.

"I don't know. You haven't said, and you seem to keep things under wraps around people. Neither of us is really looking for anything serious, I thought."

He runs a hand through his hair, "Lilly, so help me God, if you think for one second that I only want you in my bed, then you're dead wrong. As soon as this weather clears up, I'm taking you out properly. We're going to this party, together. I want you to be my girl. Tell me you want that, too."

His eyes plead with me, and part of me wonders if anyone would miss us if we showed up a bit late. I give my brain a mental shake and focus on the conversation at hand.

"I don't share," I tell him.

"Good, neither do I."

"I drive a semi-truck, so this means I'm gone a week or more at a time."

"I'm well aware. I plan to put roots down here in Rock Springs."

"I'm well aware," I repeat his words back to him.

"I know you've been hesitating to settle down here, but I'm willing to take this chance if you are." His eyes run over my face, looking for the slightest hint of what I'm thinking.

I'm not sure what I'm thinking. I want to try with Mike, but I'm not sure my heart could handle it when he walks away. I'm not sure I want to dig too deep into what I'm feeling, because it's so strong.

"You ready to do this?" He asks me, recapturing my attention.

I guess it's time to take the leap.

"I'm ready if you are."

"Thank God." He pulls me in for another kiss that ends far too soon. Then, we head out to his truck and to the other side of the ranch. The guys have been plowing the roads on the ranch, so people can get through, making it a pretty easy drive.

The winding driveway is almost out of a fairy tale with snow covering every inch. It gives off a magical feel. Light from the truck and the moon glisten and bounce off the snow, and my eyes are glued to the scenery. Stepping out of the truck, it doesn't feel like Texas anymore.

As we walk in, I notice Riley propped up in a chaise lounge with her feet up, like the doctor ordered, and Blaze is right beside her with his hand resting on her belly.

He's been doing that more and more, as she gets closer to her due date. Riley told me he likes to play games and try to tickle the baby. He can't wait to be a dad, and it shows.

"Want something to drink?" Mike asks.

"Sure, just some soda."

He makes his way towards the kitchen, as I look around the room. Helen and Tim's house is done up for Christmas. Where the other ranch house is decorated in red and silver, this one is decorated in blue and silver with lots of white and glitter to give off a magical effect.

I glance around and see a few people from town are here too, and it just goes to show

how much this family is loved.

Megan is talking to Anna Mae, and Hunter is standing behind Megan with his arms around her waist, and his hands resting on her baby bump that's just starting to show. He's there and ready to protect them both from any incoming threats, like spilled drinks, and I laugh to myself.

Royce is standing next to Anna Mae, soaking up every word she says. I hope that girl opens her eyes soon because that boy is head over heels for her. Anyone with a set of eyes can see.

Jason and Ella are talking with her parents and off to the side. Maggie is chatting with Nick, Jason's friend, and the chef at WJ's.

I walk around the outside of the room and stop when I see Mike talking to Colt, and I stop to enjoy the sight of Mike. He's tall, and the way his jeans hug his ass should be illegal. I'm thinking so hard about our conversation, before we came over, that I don't notice him walking over to me.

"You know, you're standing under the mistletoe," he looks up, and I follow his eyes. Sure enough, there's mistletoe over my head.

When I look back at Mike, he sets our drinks down on the table near us, and then his hands are on my cheeks, framing my face. I look at his lips then back to his mouth, and in the next moment, his lips are on mine.

Right there in front of everyone, he kisses me, and you know that moment everyone talks about where fireworks go off? I feel it, but it's like the fireworks are being shot up and down my body.

His lips are soft and warm and dance across mine like that's what they were meant to do. He angles my head just right, deepening the kiss before he pulls away.

When he backs up, I'm breathless and fighting to catch my breath. He's breathing just as hard. I notice everyone around us staring. Embarrassed, I bolt out to the back porch to catch my breath.

He's a few steps behind me.

"Lilly, are you okay?"

I'm not sure if I am or not. That was the most intense kiss of my life, and everyone I know was watching. There's no hiding us now or going back, and I know as soon as I go back into that room, there will be tons of questions for both of us.

Even with all that, I can't stop thinking about that kiss.

"My mom always said, when there are sparks during a mistletoe kiss, it's because two soul mates have been brought together by Christmas magic."

I turn and look him in eye.

"I felt it, too," he whispers.

I nod and stare out over the snow. "I meant it, Lilly. I want this, us. I want everyone to know, and while it's a little late now, we can go back in there and act like there's nothing between us, if that's what you want."

"And you'd be okay with that?"

"I'd find a way to be okay with it," he pauses. "For you."

Is that what I want? To pretend like it never happened. I don't think I could pretend no matter how hard I tried.

"I don't want to act like there's nothing between us, but I also don't want to go back inside."

He reaches into his pocket and pulls out his truck key. "Head to the truck, and I'll grab our stuff, and then we can go talk at my place for a bit, yeah?"

I nod and take the keys. As I make my way to the truck, I notice I ran outside without my coat. When I get in the truck, I crank up the heat. I'd still rather battle the cold then go back inside there tonight.

He meets me back at the truck a minute later with our coats, and we drive in silence to his cabin. Once inside, he watches me, like he's waiting for me to go off. Finally, I break the silence.

"You believe what your mom said about the mistletoe kiss?"

"I've seen it happen many times. She and my dad, my grandparents, and my cousin."

My heart pounds thinking about that kiss. So much so, that I don't notice he's in front of me until his body is pressed to mine. Ever so slowly, he leans in, and his lips find mine. It's a soft and gentle kiss like he's waiting for permission to take it further.

I reach up and wrap my arms around his neck, pulling him into me. He deepens the kiss, and I barely feel my back hitting the wall, or his lips crushing into mine, as we explore each other.

"If you are going to stop me, do it now, Lilly. I don't think I'll be able to stop after much longer. I want you too much." Mike's deep timber reaches my ears, turning me on even more.

"I don't want you to stop." My voice is wobbly, even as I try to keep it steady.

His eyes meet mine, and at that moment, time stands still, and nothing else matters. Not my job, not the snow outside, and not everything that should be keeping us apart.

It's just us and this moment.

He reaches for the hem of my dress, and then slowly peels it off of me. His eyes trace every inch that's exposed, until his eyes land back on mine.

My turn. I run my hand down his chest and under his shirt, and I don't miss the bulge in his pants. I lightly brush it, as I unbutton his shirt, and his groan makes me want to smile.

I take my time unbuttoning his shirt, before sliding it off his shoulders, exposing the hard cowboy muscle underneath. The tan skin and defined muscles you can only get from hard work, and they are a breathtaking sight. I could stand here and appreciate his body all night.

I run my hands over his shoulders, and then slowly down his chest, watching his muscles ripple under my fingers. When I get to the chiseled abs, I let my hands trail down the ridges, and then down to the happy trail that I can't wait to follow. The sound of his breathing quickens, and he groans when my hand drifts to the top of his pants.

Looking up at him from under my lashes, I see him watching my hands. This spurs me on to rub over his tenting jeans before I unbutton and unzip them.

I run my hands back up his chest and around his neck, pulling him into another kiss, as he makes quick work of shedding his jeans.

"Hold on, firecracker." He says as he pulls my legs around his hips, grabbing a hold of my ass. He carries me over to the couch and lays me down. He runs his hands up my back and unclasps my bra. Slowly sliding his hands around to the front of my chest, he sends my bra flying.

As he sits back and looks at me, the desire on his face turns me on even more, if that's even possible. He gently runs his thumbs over my already hard nipples, before sliding his hands down to my barely there dark, red lace panties.

"I really like these." He runs his finger over the hem, before pulling them down. He stands and sheds his black, boxer briefs, before reaching for his pants. He pulls a condom out of his wallet and tosses his wallet on the coffee table, before making his way back over to me.

He kneels down in front of the couch, and in a quick movement, flips me to sit up, pulling my ass to the edge of the couch. He tosses my legs over his shoulders, and before I can even get a word out, his mouth is on my clit. He's doing that thing with his tongue that drives me crazy, and I couldn't stop the moans if I tried.

He's already learned how to play my body like a fiddle, and in no time, he has me on the verge of a climax. He pulls away to look up at me, as I let out a frustrated whine that makes him smirk.

He leans in, never taking his eyes off mine, and lazily licks me.

"Mike, please!" I gasp.

"Please, what? I love hearing your words."

"Please, make me cum!"

He increases his efforts, and in no time, my body locks up, as the climax he's been building, washes over me.

"I love that my firecracker goes off just like fireworks. Gives your name a whole new meaning." He jokes. Then licking his lips, he reaches for the condom and quickly rolls it on.

Before I've caught my breath, he's laying me down on the couch carefully, like I'm breakable. This rough cowboy being so gentle with me overwhelms my senses, and before he can see my eyes mist over, I pull him back in for another kiss.

He settles himself over me, while never breaking the kiss. The head of his cock presses against my pussy lips, and I gasp. He locks eyes with mine, as he slowly slides into me. He stretches me, slowly rocking himself in and out until he's fully seated inside me.

"So tight. So perfect. So mine." He whispers as he sets a steady rhythm. When he leans down to kiss me again, it's not the gentle kiss from before. This one is full of need, and it's about dominance and passion.

Without breaking the kiss, and without warning, he pulls me up, so I'm seated against his hips, and he's kneeling on the couch. My front is plastered to his front, as he continues thrusting in and out of me.

His hand tangles in my hair, deepening the kiss, while my nipples rub against his coarse chest hair. My skin tingles with hundreds of tiny sparks that shoot straight to my core.

It's sensation overload, and when he switches the angle of his hips, it sets me over the edge, screaming his name. Wave after wave rushes through me, and his loud grunt fills my ears, before he crushes me to him, as his body shakes in pleasure.

Neither of us moves for a few minutes, while we catch our breath. My head is buried in his neck, and I can't remember the last time I ever felt so relaxed.

"Hold on tight, baby." He whispers in my ear, and I hold on, as he carries us back to the bedroom.

He gently lays me on his bed and pulls the covers over me. He disappears into the bathroom to clean up and comes out with a wet washcloth and cleans me up as well.

When he's done, he climbs into bed and pulls me against his chest.

"I was never one to cuddle, but with you, I don't want to stop." He whispers in my ear.

Wrapped in his warmth and more comfortable than I've ever have been, it doesn't take long to fall asleep.

This gentle side of him is new and steals more of my heart, making me want to stay permanently in Rock Springs.

Chapter 13

I sneak back into my bedroom the next day before everyone wakes up, and I find Riley wide awake in my bed, reading a magazine.

She looks at me and sets the magazine down.

"So, you didn't come home last night, huh?"

I cringe. "No."

"Close the door and sit down. It's time we talk."

I shut the door and join her on the bed, but she speaks first.

"Everyone saw that kiss, Lil. It was hot."

I can feel the blush creep across my face.

"Yeah, it was." I agree.

I look down at my hands in my lap.

"So, where did you go?"

"Mike and I left. We talked a bit, had sex, and I spent the night."

"What!" Riley screeches.

"Calm down, before Blaze comes butting in here!"

Riley takes a deep breath. "Was that your first kiss with him?"

"No." I go on to tell her about being trapped in the cabin during the rain, and how I've been spending every night in his bed. I share about our conversation, before going into the party, and then the conversation after.

"Do you want a relationship with him?" Riley asks.

"Yes, but, how can I? I'm on the road as much as I'm off, and it kills a relationship. The last two guys couldn't handle it. They lost trust in me and thought I was always cheating because I keep odd hours on the road."

"Oh, I know what." Riley smiles. "You don't think you owe it to yourself to at least try, but you should know, the right guy will trust you."

"I don't know if my heart can take it. I really like him, Riles. I mean really, really, really like him. I don't think I could take it if it didn't work out, because of my job."

She nods, "Plus, you live in Tulsa."

"Ahhh, not anymore. I sold my place and put my things in storage right before you landed on bed rest."

Riley is quiet, as she stares at me. "Why?"

"Well, I don't have anything holding me there. I was never happy when I was there and always itching to get back on the road. Home should be a place I can't wait to get back to and don't want to leave."

"And where is that, Lilly?"

"I'm starting to think it's here in Rock Springs."

"I was hoping it is. I want you here."

"Dave called me today. I'm delayed a few more days, before getting back on the road. I'm thinking of calling and using up more vacation time, sticking around for the holiday."

"I think you should."

"Really?" I'm a bit shocked. I thought she'd say I should get back to my life and see how Mike fits in. That's what I was thinking I should do.

"Selfishly, I want you around more, but if you think this is home, you need to decide. It sounds like you don't want to get back on the road."

"Not really. For the first time in six years, I'm dreading it."

"So, take some of that vacation time, and then decide what you want to do."

"Okay."

"Call Dave now. I know he's up early just like you are."

I smile and pull out my phone. My nerves hit because I know this is a busy time, but I never ask for time off. I guess the worst he can say is no. He already promised me that I can be here until the baby is born, so I have that to look forward to.

"Hey, Dave."

"Lilly, I was just going to call you with an update."

"About that, you were right. I did need this vacation, and I was hoping to use up some more of my time through Christmas if that's okay?"

"Damnit, Lilly. If it were anyone else asking this time of year, then I'd say no." He pauses, and I can picture him rubbing his forehead like he does when he's thinking. "If anyone asks, you tell them you are so snowed in and you can't get out, you hear me?"

"Yes, sir."

"Enjoy being snowed in, Lilly. You deserve the break."

I hang up, smiling at Riley, and instantly, it's like a weight is lifted off my shoulders.

"Feel better already, don't you?"

"Yeah."

"Now, Sage got a call last night that Abby is coming in to spend Christmas break with them between classes, and she flies into Dallas tomorrow. You have the most experience in this type of weather, and Colt's truck is the best equipped. Would you be willing to go pick her up?"

Abby is Sage's friend, who stayed at the ranch after her parents died last year. She moved to go to school in Arkansas, and now, she comes back every chance she gets.

"And bring back peppermint bark and donuts," I tease.

"God yes, please!"

I laugh. "I'd be happy, too."

"Perfect! Everyone promised not to hound you if you talked to me. I will send out a peace order. You go get ready and head down for breakfast."

"Gee, thanks." I pause, "Hey, Riley?"

"Yeah?"

"Can we not tell anyone I'm staying through Christmas just yet? I want to see how this plays out."

"Of course."

I get ready and head downstairs. I grab some breakfast and sit at the table with Hunter and Megan. I was going to mind my own business and hurry and eat, so I could get to the barn when they catch my attention.

"I was at my parents' place, and the ranch next door just went up for sale," Hunter says.

"Oh, The McCall's have lived there forever," Megan nods a little sadly.

"Yeah, but I guess they want to move to Florida," Hunter says.

"How big is the ranch?" I ask.

"About 300 acres, and it's just a bit smaller than my parents' place. It has a stable, a bunkhouse, and a few cabins on it. Because of the creek that runs through it, it's got some good wildlife, and it's perfect for hunting in the fall."

It sounds like it has everything Mike needs and wants. I have to go into Dallas tomorrow, so I can swing by and take a look before I get his hopes up.

"Any idea on the condition of the buildings?"

"They're kept up pretty well. I'm sure the house needs updating since she was a fan of the 80's shag carpet the last time I was there," Hunter says.

"Didn't you say at one point your mom used to take in abused horses?" I ask him.

"Yeah, and any other kind of animal that needed a home. Why, what's on your mind?"

He asks.

"Just thinking." I smile. This might be the sign I've been looking for.

• • • • ● • ● • ● • • •

"Lilly!" Abby runs up and hugs me. That's one thing about Abby. She greets you like you are sisters and the best of friends. She just got off the plane and looks amazing. We've met a few times in passing, and she has always been sweet.

"Abby! How was your flight?"

"Boring," she laughs.

"Okay, so I have a secret mission. I'm hoping you won't mind a detour on the way home, but we have to keep it quiet."

"Oh, I love secret missions. My lips are sealed."

"First, peppermint bark and donuts."

"Oh, yes. Riley texted telling me not to let you forget them," she laughs.

"I would never!" I gasp in fake shock, causing us both to erupt in giggles, as we make our way out to Colt's truck that he let me borrow for the trip.

Once we have the peppermint bark and donuts, we head back towards Rock Springs.

"Alright, now tell me what our mission is," Abby turns in her seat to watch me.

"Well, yesterday Hunter mentioned the ranch next to his parents went up for sale. I know someone who is in the market for a ranch, but I don't want to get his hopes up in case it's not a fit. He's been looking for a while and hasn't had much luck. So, I wanted to stop by and look on our way home. I set up an appointment and everything."

"This someone wouldn't be Mike, would it?"

"I swear Riley is the biggest gossip in that house," I say.

"Well, she's so bored on bed rest. You know, she begged me to come down between exams."

"Yeah, she begged me, too," I admit. "She talked me in to staying for Christmas, and even made me think it was my idea until I got a chance to think it over."

We talk a bit about her midwife classes, and the family she's staying with on our way to the ranch. When we pull up, Ryan is there.

"You must be Ryan," I ask.

"Yeah, Lilly, right?"

"Yes, and this is my friend Abby. I know you've talked with Mike and his dad about properties and all."

"I promised you, Lilly. Not a word that you've been here."

"Thanks. Now, let's take a look around."

We spend an hour looking at the property. It has not one but two bunkhouses, which would be perfect for campers, a boy's and a girl's bunk. There's also a large foreman's house, which would make a great staff house.

The stables can hold twenty horses and have a nice office, too. Ryan tells us they can be expanded pretty easily as needed. The main house is set far enough from the other buildings for privacy, even though it does need some updating. While I'm standing here, I can picture us in the house.

Sunday breakfast, dinner every night, and someday kids running around. Standing in the house, it hits me. This is where I want to be, and this is what I want to do. I've been scared to admit how much I love Mike's dream because I didn't think I could be a part of it. Now, I see it, and I want it, but more importantly, I want it for him.

This is worth putting it all on the line for. This is worth getting off the road and putting down roots. Now to make him believe it. With a look at Abby, I start to plan the biggest Christmas miracle anyone in the state of Texas has seen.

"Remember, not a word," I tell Abby.

"Promise. If they ask about what took so long, I'll say there was a line at the bakery, and then we took it slow, because of the snow."

"Should I be worried about how well you can lie?" I ask her.

"No, my mom loved surprises, so my dad and I became good at being able to hide things, so we could pull them off."

I nod. Her parents died in a car crash earlier this year, and she stayed on the ranch, before moving in with a family in Arkansas, so she could go to school to become a midwife. Her parents owned a bed and breakfast in Memphis, and Sage went up and helped her sell it. There was some drama with the church her parents belonged to, trying to take control of the B&B, but I don't remember the details.

Abby seems to have bounced back and is doing well. She's bubbly and full of light, so I guess she's on the right path.

On the drive back to the ranch, my mind is whirling a million miles a minute of everything I need to get done, and how I'm going to be able to do it in secret.

Once we get to the ranch, I head out to make a few calls and put my plan in motion.

Chapter 14

I'm watching Lilly and Abby brush down Kit Kat and can't pull my eyes away. Lilly fits in so well here, and Abby jumped right in, even though she arrived yesterday.

I finally tear my eyes away, when Blaze walks up beside me, nodding towards the office.

"So, you and Lilly?" He asks once the door closes behind me.

"Yeah, she's it for me, and I feel it in my gut. She's my Riley," I tell him.

His whole face softens. "Does she know that?"

"I told her I'm serious about us, and that I wasn't going anywhere. I just don't want to scare her off with how deep that runs."

"What about her job? She's always on the road," Blaze asks.

"Her job isn't an issue for me. She seems to love it, and if it's what makes her happy, how can I get in the way of that. Do I love the idea of her being gone so much? No, but can you blame me? But I do know, I'll find a way to make it work."

Blaze is silent, before he asks, "So, what now?"

"Now, it's time to convince her how I feel, so there's no doubt in her head when she gets back on the road."

"If you want this bad enough, you'll be able to do it."

He pats me on the shoulder and heads out of the office. I decide to get some ordering and paperwork done before I go look for Lilly.

This time I find her cleaning out her rig and putting all her stuff in boxes.

"What're you doing?" I ask her.

"Oh, hey, Mike. Just the person I was hoping to see. I need a favor," she smiles at me. I wonder if she knows she could get me to do anything she wants with that smile.

"What's up?" I ask.

"Well, I have to take my rig up to Amarillo to the main shop. I decided to stick around through Christmas, so they want to do some work on it over the break. I was hoping you'd follow me up, so I have a ride back. If we leave early, we can do it in a day."

A whole day with her? There's no way I'm turning that down. I'll find a way to make it work. In my mind, I'm already rearranging things and planning who to ask to pick up a few chores.

"Of course. When do you need to get it up there?"

"Day after tomorrow."

"Done."

She leans in and kisses my cheek. "Thank you, Mike."

I watch her head back into her rig and finish pulling stuff out. I'm already working out what I need to do to make it happen, and also, trying to see if I can squeeze in a proper date on the way.

• • • • • • • • • •

Lilly

"Are you sure you want to do this?" Dave asks as I'm standing in the trucking office, getting ready to sign the paperwork to end my employment with Dave and his company. With the paperwork completed, I'll get the rest of my vacation time in a lump sum payment.

He gave me a job right out of school and taught me everything I know. I have been loyal to him, and he hasn't ignored that fact. Part of me feels like I'm letting him down, but in my heart, I know this is the right thing to do.

We drove up to Amarillo today, and I just walked into the office. Mike is waiting in his truck, thinking I'm turning my keys in, so they can do maintenance on my truck. I don't like lying to him or anyone, but it's for the best right now.

This will be the last time I'm here as an employee, and it just feels right. As I was packing up my stuff from the rig, I thought I'd be sad, but I wasn't. I felt at peace about my decision, and that's why I have no regrets now.

I was expecting tears on the drive here, thinking about it being my last time in the rig that has been my home away from home, but none came. That's how I know I'm making the right choice. I still pause and think it over one more time.

The thought of getting back on the road makes my stomach sink, but the thought of staying in Rock Springs, makes me happy, and I have butterflies in my stomach, thinking of the possibilities in front of me.

"I'm sure, Dave. I've been trying to figure out my next steps for a while, and now, I finally have."

"I'm really regretting making you take a break. If you had stayed on the road, none of this would have happened." He tries to sound upset, but there's a huge smile on his face. "At least, tell me there's a guy involved. You know my wife is going to ask."

"Of course, there is," I laugh.

"Okay, well if you change your mind and come back here, then I'll always have a spot for you. You're one of my top drivers, better than half the guys here, and I hate to lose you, but I understand needing to put down roots, too. It's why I got off the road and started the company," Dave says, as I finish signing the papers.

"I promise, if I decide to get behind the wheel of a rig again, there's no one I'd rather work for."

He comes around the counter, handing me the check with my last paycheck and vacation pay. I also notice my Christmas bonus check is in the envelope. I thought I was forfeiting this by quitting before Christmas.

"Dave, you know I haven't even worked this month!"

"I know, but even with your break, you have put more miles on the books than anyone this year. All your deliveries have been on time, you have no traffic violations, and the only damage you had was when that drunk guy backed into your rig at the hotel in Denver. You more than earned that bonus, and I'm not cheating you out of it."

I have to hug Dave, and while it's an awkward hug, he hugs me back.

"Thank you. This is going to be a huge help for my plans."

"Good, now go get your cowboy. I'm guessing he's the one in the truck, looking rather impatient out there."

"Yeah, that's him," I smile.

"Keep in touch, Lilly."

"You too, Dave."

I head out to meet Mike with a huge smile on my face. When he sees me walking towards him, a big smile overtakes his face, too.

When I get into the truck, his hand goes to the back of my neck, pulling me in for a quick kiss, and then he nods at the envelope in my hand.

"Everything okay?" He asks.

"Yeah, this is just my Christmas bonus. I guess I put more miles on the books than anyone else at the company this year, so it was more than I was expecting." I say as I tuck the envelope into my bag.

"I'm proud of you, Lilly, and you're an amazing driver, too. They say what needs to be done on your rig?" He asks as he points the truck towards home.

"Well, since I'm going to be off, they'll go over the engine with a fine-tooth comb, make sure everything is working, change the fluids, belts, and clean everything up." I hate lying to him, but it's not really a lie. They'll do all that work before they give it to the next driver.

Not even the thought of someone else driving my rig puts a damper on my mood.

"Hey, there's a great diner a few exits up. We should stop for lunch. If you want me to drive home, I can. It's a long day if you aren't used to driving it," I tell him.

"Yes to the food, and no, I want you to relax. I promise I'm good to drive. Much better now that you're in the truck with me."

He looks over for a brief moment and smiles at me, before pulling his eyes back to the road. A field of butterflies takes up in my stomach. It's a sensation I don't remember feeling, since I was a kid when I'd ride those roller coasters with the steep drops.

We stop and grab lunch, and it's great to just be out and carefree. Mike is nothing short of a perfect gentleman, holding the door open for me and pulling out my chair. He didn't even seem to notice when the waitress tried to flirt with him, because he always had his eyes on me, when she was around.

Once back in the truck and heading home, my phone rings, and I'm more than shocked to see it's my sister.

"Vanna?" I answer.

"Lilly!" She giggles.

"Everything okay? Are *you* okay?" I'm hesitant because it's been a while, since we talked, and I know she has the big tour to prepare for. I also see Mike watching me, ready to jump in and help if needed. His protective side seems to be slipping out more and more.

"Yes! More than okay! So, you know I got that opening spot on the tour, right?"

"Yes. I'm so happy for you. I bet it's going to be a ton of fun, too."

"It's a lot of work, too. Anyway, they gave everyone the rest of the year off to spend with family, before getting back together for the tour. I was hoping you'd let me come out there and spend some time with you before I head to see Mom and Dad for Christmas," she asks, sounding nervous.

"Vanna! I'd love to have you here! When will you be here? I'll pick you up at the airport. Riley will love another reason for me to head to Dallas and get more peppermint bark and donuts!"

"Well, if the weather holds, I was looking at coming in on Monday and staying a week."

"Of course! Send me your flight info, and I'll be at the airport. I can't wait to see you."

"I can't wait either. I miss you, tiger. See you Monday."

She hangs up, and I let out a little squeal, making Mike laugh.

"Good news, I take it."

"Yes! My sister is coming to spend a week with me. Oh, Mike. I haven't seen her in a year. She just got signed to open a huge tour, and I didn't think she'd get away before it started. They're giving everyone the rest of the year off. So, she's coming to spend time with me, before leaving to spend Christmas with Mom and Dad."

Mike glances over at me, "You going to spend Christmas with them, too?"

"No, I'm here for Riley, and I don't want to chance her going into labor early and missing it. I already talked to Mom and Dad, and they understand."

We spend the rest of the truck ride home, talking about my sister and all the funny stories of her and me growing up. I don't think I realized until now how much I missed her since she got her record deal.

Chapter 15

I'm daydreaming about everything I still have to get done for Mike's Christmas surprise when a loud voice breaks through my mental fog.

"Tiger Lilly!" Then, a hard body crashes into me.

"Vanna!" She hugs me so tight that I'm finding it hard to breathe. "I missed you," I grunt out before she finally lets me go.

She's dressed down in jeans, a t-shirt, and boots with her long, brown hair pulled back in a messy bun. Even walking off an airplane, she looks like she could walk right on stage.

A few people have stared, and I'm pretty sure at least one girl recognizes her because she has her phone out.

"Come on, let's head out to the car, and I can tell you about this peppermint bark." I take her bag and leave the airport.

Once we have our peppermint bark and donuts, and we are on the road to Rock Springs, Savannah goes right for my throat.

"Okay, what's going on? Mom and Dad said you're staying in Rock Springs, and they said you met a guy. I want the sister version since we have time. Fess up."

"Well, after you, Mom, and Dad left Tulsa, it just didn't feel like home, so I knew I'd needed to find where I wanted to be. I think that night I picked Riley up was just as much her fate as it was mine. Rock Springs feels like home. I have friends there, and yeah, I met Mike. The more we talked, the more I fell in love with his dream of owning a ranch, as a camp to rehab horses and work with kids."

"You don't know a thing about ranching, tiger," she says.

"I didn't, but I've learned so much. My experience with engines has helped tremendously, and you'll see Riley's family is always willing to teach. I've soaked it all up. Vanna, I found the perfect property for Mike."

"What does he think of it?"

"I haven't told him. I..." I hesitate because this will be the first time I'm speaking about my plans out loud. Heck, the first time I will be voicing them to the universe.

"You what?" She pushes me. I know she won't let it go. Even as a kid, she'd be like a dog with a bone at the first hint of anything. When she got a hint of a bone, she pulled it from you.

"I want to buy it, and then surprise him with it."

She lets out a long, slow whistle, and then stares out of the window.

"So, this isn't just some guy you're seeing. This is *the* guy. He's the one, isn't he?"

"He kissed me under the mistletoe, and I've never had sparks like that. And I knew before then, that there was some magic there."

"Well, I want to see this property, while I'm here. If you're so sure about it, then I have to see it."

"Okay, I'll call the realtor and set up a time. Do you... Do you think he will get upset if I keep this from him and surprise him?"

"Maybe a little, but once he sees what you really did for him, I'm sure it won't matter. Lilly, this is big, and if this is your dream, I want to help. You helped me and pushed me to sing, and you're always helping other people. I got a huge signing bonus, so please, let me help with the down payment," her voice is soft, so I know she's serious.

"Vanna, that bonus is for you. You worked hard for it, and you should spoil yourself."

She waves her hand at me, "I'm single, I got a new car, a small condo for when I'm in town, killer shoes, and a new phone. I paid off the mortgage for Mom and Dad's condo in Sedona, when I got my first big check for the record. Now, I want to spoil you, and I won't take no for an answer. You let me do this, Lilly," her voice is stern, and it reminds me of when she would demand I play tea party with her, instead of heading to Dad's shop to help him out.

I smile at her. "Fine, but it stays a secret. I want to surprise Mike."

She giggles and stomps her feet on the floor.

"Now your turn. Tell me about this tour."

"Oh, Lilly! It's with the band, *Three Stevens*, which is very confusing when you're talking to them. We were calling them Steven the singer, or Steven the drummer, so we gave them nicknames. The drummer is called Pickles, and there's a story there, but I'll spare you the details. The guitarist is nicknamed Bass, and the lead singer, we call him Thunder, because of his voice. When those first few notes fill the room, it's like thunder rolling in. They are down to earth and good guys.

They're all married, and they're talking of bringing their wives on the tour. It'll be nice to have other girls on the bus."

She goes on to tell me about some of the songs they have been working on, and the props for the stage. She relates some of the behind the scenes stuff, and it's exciting how passionate she is.

As we turn into the ranch, her eyes go big. "Wow, this place is huge. I can see its appeal."

Sage greats Savannah, like she's known her forever, and before I even get out of the truck, she whisks her away to get her set up in a guest room.

"I don't know how much more time you'll get with her now," the husky voice jokes. I don't even have to turn around, because I know his voice anywhere.

"Yeah, I can't wait for you to meet her. She knows all about us, and I'm sure she won't go easy on you." I turn and meet Mike's eyes.

"Good. I don't want her to. I want her to know without a shadow of a doubt I'll take care of you and for her to see how good we are together," he says, while not breaking eye contact.

His arms wrap around my waist, as he pulls me in for a kiss. His soft lips dance across mine, before pulling away all too soon.

"You better go rescue her from Sage," he smacks my ass, as he takes a step back. "And Lilly?"

I turn to look at him but don't say a word.

"Spend time with your sister, while she's here, and don't worry about coming to the cabin. I'll be here when she leaves," he winks and then turns, walking into the barn.

I watch him go. There's something about watching a cowboy walking away in chaps that does something to a girl. You have to stop and fully appreciate the view. I shake my head and turn to head into the house. I'm not going to go a week without him. I can't go a week without him, which strikes me as crazy, because I used to do longer stretches than that on the road.

•••••••••••

"Lilly, it's beautiful! I can see you here, and maybe even with some nieces and nephews running around," Savannah gushes, as we stand on the front porch of the property I'm working to buy for Mike. "This sells it. I'm helping you. I haven't seen you smile this much in so long. You've only smiled like this around Mike, and since we have been on this property." She hugs me, and I know now that once she has a plan in her head, there's no stopping her.

She's been here three days, and she's already wearing boots and flannel and trying to fit in. She loves being around the horses as much as I do and has been helping Sage with some of her training. She and Sage have bonded pretty well. Then again, everyone loves Sage, because she's so friendly and welcomes you like she's known you her entire life.

Vanna even took a few shifts of sitting with Riley. Even though, I know she shared all my childhood stories with her. I love seeing them getting along so well, too. Knowing my sister fits in with my friends here, is just another sign I'm where I'm meant to be.

As I stand on the porch, I too see my life here with Mike by my side. Mike, whose bed I haven't been in for three nights now, and who I miss like crazy. Savannah is going to bed early tonight because she has a few morning phone calls with her manager, so I'm sneaking out to see Mike.

It's all I can think about all day. He seems just as desperate for me, because every chance he gets, he's pulling me in for a quick kiss or pressing me up in some dark corner for a long passionate kiss. It has me so wet and needing him. My skin is on fire, so much so, I feel like I could walk around without a jacket in all this snow, and never once feel the cold.

After Savannah goes to bed, I head right out to Mike's cabin and don't bother knocking. Until now, he has been leaving the door unlocked, and I would just slip in when I could get away. I do the same tonight and find him leaning against his kitchen counter with a glass of water in hand.

He sets the glass down and stalks towards me silently, until he's standing in front of me, pressing me up against the door

"You should be spending time with your sister." His voice is gruff, as he grips my hips.

"She's asleep, and I couldn't sleep," I whisper.

"Is that right?" His eyes trail over my face and down my neck.

I nod ever so slightly, and in the next moment, his lips are on mine in a frenzy, showing me, he missed me as much as I missed him. The thought of not spending the night with him tonight was just too much.

He makes quick work of pulling off my shirt and his.

"Need you skin to skin." He grunts out, before pushing me back against the door and melting our bodies together in another soul searing kiss.

This time is softer, but he pours the need into it, as he undoes my jeans. While I step out of them, he pulls his wallet out, grabs a condom, and undresses himself. I remove my bra and underwear, as I watch him put the condom on.

"I feel like I should drag this out and tease you for hours, but I need you so much." He runs a finger through my slit, finding me wet, and groans. "It looks like you need me just as much."

He brings his finger to his mouth, and then grabs my hips, lifting me up against the door. I wrap my arms around his neck and my legs around his hips, as he slides into me.

We both groan with his forehead on mine, as he starts a slow thrust that picks up speed. Soon, he's at a hurried pace, slamming into me, and it's all I can do to hold on to my muscular cowboy.

He pushes me into the door, and his hand trails along my hip, until his thumb is rubbing against my clit.

"I want to watch you come, Lilly." He breathes out, never breaking his pace.

He plays my clit so well that I come before I can even answer him. He doesn't let up until I relax, and then he pulls me against him, carrying me to the bedroom. He lays me down in his bed, before crawling over me.

He slides back into me and pauses to brace himself on his elbows. He runs his hands through my hair slowly under my head. It's relaxing and sends sparks down my spine.

His eyes meet mine, and his cock starts pushing into me slowly, leisurely our bodies slick with sweat. This time is different. It's more than the hurried sex against the door. This time means more, and his eyes are telling me everything he can't say.

He leans down and lightly kisses my jaw and my neck, before reaching the top of my breasts. Using one hand, he brings it to his mouth, running his tongue over my stiff nipple, before sucking it into his mouth, causing me to gasp. He keeps his thrusts slow and matches his tongue on my nipple to the pace of his thrusts. He turns and gives my other nipple the same attention, driving me crazy.

I wrap my legs around his hips, trying to pull him closer, as he's kissing me. The tender mixed with a hard thrust, it's my undoing. I cum again, my body locking up.

"Lilly!" Mike roars, as his whole body tenses. He gasps for air, before rolling to the side and pulling me close to him.

"I'm so glad you didn't stay away tonight. I've gotten too used to sleeping with you tucked against me that I was having problems sleeping." Mike whispers against my hair before he gets up to clean us both.

I watch him climb back into bed. All tan muscle and rough cowboy.

"Like what you see?" He smirks, catching me watching.

I snuggle up to him, once he's under the covers. "Very much so."

"Good, your opinion is the only one I care about. Now, go to sleep. I got you."

He pulls me in tight, and with his body heat surrounding me and the safety of his arms, sleep isn't far behind.

Chapter 16

L oud pounding wakes me up, but I'm instantly calmed by the arms wrapped around me. I snuggle back into Mike, soaking up his warmth. I missed sleeping in his arms with Savannah here. She headed out to visit Mom and Dad yesterday, and I've been back in his bed, right where I belong. I'm just getting comfortable when there's another loud knock on the door.

"Damnit, Lilly. I know you're in there. Open up!" Sage's voice calls.

We both jump out of bed and pull on some clothes before I open the door. I don't even get a word out before Sage jumps in.

"Yes, everyone knows you sneak out here, and it's not a big deal. Riley is in labor, and she's asking for you," Sage says, and then turns, running back towards the house.

"Shit," I say, grabbing my coat and boots. Beside me, Mike gets dressed, too.

"Guess the cat's out of the bag, huh?" He jokes. "Come on, let's get you over to the main house."

When we walk in, it's a flurry of activity you don't expect at one a.m. Even Blaze and Sage's parents, Helen and Tim, are here. I assume they just got here, as they are taking off their coats, too.

"What's the update?" Helen asks.

"Abby is up there now, and the contractions are pretty regular every six to seven minutes, and Blaze is calling their doctor now," Megan tells us.

"I was told to send Lilly up," Colt comes walking down the stairs, looking for me.

I squeeze Mike's hand and head upstairs to Riley's room. I pause and take a deep breath outside the door before knocking.

"Lilly!" Riley runs over and hugs me. I look over her shoulder to see Blaze, hanging up the phone.

"The doctor said we should get to the hospital. She wants to check on you herself."

"Okay, Lilly will drive us. Blaze, my bag is packed in the closet. Sage, you direct whoever else is coming. Everyone is welcome, and there's a huge family waiting room, but only a few, will be in my birthing room," Riley says, firing off instructions.

"Is she okay to be walking?" I ask Blaze since she was still supposed to be on bed rest.

"Doctor didn't say, but good luck stopping her," he tries to smile, but I see the concern in his eyes.

We all file downstairs when another contraction hits Riley halfway down the staircase. She leans on me, while Blaze rubs her lower back, and Abby makes note of the contraction times. Once it passes, we load up.

"Hey, call me and let me know how it goes," Mike says, giving me a quick kiss.

"No, I expect you in the waiting room with me. Please?" His hand runs through my hair, and he kisses my forehead.

"Anything for you. I'll be there."

Once Riley is settled, we make our way to the hospital. Halfway there, she has a really strong contraction.

"Do I need to pull over?" I ask more to Abby than anyone.

"So help me Lilly, if you pull over, and I have this baby on the side of the road, I'll strangle you with the umbilical cord!" Riley yells back. The threat is enough to make me speed up to get her to the hospital quickly.

When we get in, they whisk Riley, Blaze, and Sage away to the room, and a nice nurse shows us to the family waiting room. Thankfully, Mike and the rest of the family were right behind us. I collapse on the couch next to Mike, resting my head on his shoulder.

"Close your eyes, firecracker. I've got you," he murmurs, kissing the top of my head.

"I don't think I could sleep to save my life. I'm so wired and excited."

"We all are," Helen pats my knee. "Now that we have time on our hands, maybe it's a good time for you to tell us this story." She points between Mike and me.

I groan, "On second thought, maybe I will take that nap."

There are a few laughs coming from around the room, but Mike takes over and talks about how we met, and how it just grew until Riley asked me to stay.

"Well, I'm happy for you two and excited. This means you'll be around more," Helen says.

"I second that," Ella smiles at me. She's sitting with Jason and looking like she's fighting sleep.

Megan is curled up on Hunter's lap, looking the same way.

"Get some sleep, while you can. I'm sure we will be here a bit," Helen says like she can read my mind.

Just as everyone is getting settled, Sage comes out. "Riley is all hooked up to the monitors, and she and the baby are doing great. The doctor says we'll be having the baby today. The doctor also thinks she's sitting at seven centimeters, and the contractions are strong. Lilly, she wants you in the room."

I look over to Mike, who is smiling at me. "Go, I'll be here. I've got nothing but time." He gives me a quick kiss, and I'm off, following Sage down the halls.

"I don't know what to expect," I tell her a bit nervous.

"That makes two of us," she stops outside of a door. "Listen, Blaze is a mess. Both he and Riley need us to be strong. She's too far along to get an epidural, so she isn't too happy. Do what the nurses and the doctors ask, and let's try to keep her comfortable and calm. Anything else, just ask her nurse. She's really nice. We've got this, okay?"

I nod, and Sage hugs me. I soak up her warmth before she pulls back and opens the door.

"What took you so long!" Riley yells, her face contorted with pain.

"It's a maze of hallways out there. I took a wrong turn, but we're both here. Now, what do you need?" Sage asks.

"I want to get up on the ball," Riley points to a large yoga looking ball.

Sage and Blaze help her out of bed, and she sits on the ball, letting Blaze hold her hands, while Sage rubs her lower back.

Her face pinches, and I know another contraction is on the way.

"Deep breaths, and don't hold your breath. Breathe just like that," I say nice and calm, like the videos I watched did.

I had no idea what to expect, so I watched some TV shows on child birth to get an idea. I also watched some videos on Lamaze breathing, and now, I'm really glad I did. We help her through a few more contractions before the doctor comes in.

"Alright, Riley. Let's get you back in bed, so I can check you again, okay?" Dr. Shelly says.

Riley nods, as Blaze and I help her to bed.

"Want me to wait outside?" I ask her.

"Lilly, the three of you are not leaving this room. You're my birth team and will be here, until the end, got it?" Riley says in a firm tone, as she gets settled for the doctor.

I have tears in my eyes that she wants me here. I don't think I've ever had a friend like Riley. Without thinking twice, I lean in and hug her.

"I love you, Riley."

"I love you too, Lilly," She hugs me back. "Thank you for stopping that night and giving me this amazing life."

"Thank you for calling me that morning and inviting me along for the ride," I tell her, and we both have tears in our eyes when the doctor interrupts.

"Okay, you're at nine centimeters. I'm going to have the nurses get set up, and we should be pushing in a few minutes," she smiles, as she turns to the nurses and starts talking.

Then, there's a flurry of activity, as nurses are in and out with lights and equipment. The doctor gets ready, as a few more nurses come in.

"Okay, let's see what these last few contractions did," Dr. Shelly's says, right as Riley comes off a contraction. "Ten centimeters. Let's get to pushing!"

The doctor gives directions to Riley and talks her through it all. Riley is a champ and takes it all in stride. She chose to do it with no other pain medication, and I'm pretty sure she broke my hand, Blaze's hand, and out cursed even the worst trucker. The moment the doctor laid that baby on her belly, the shift in her was amazing to see.

I'm thankful I remembered to pull out my phone and start snapping pictures. Sage has a video going, as Riley gets to meet her new baby girl. I feel like an intruder, watching Riley and Blaze with their baby.

Blaze rests his forehead on Riley's, and they both have tears falling down their face.

"Riley..." Blaze gets choked up. "Thank you for this incredible gift, and this little girl is the most awesome thing I never thought I'd get to have."

Riley looks at him and pulls him in for a kiss. "You gave me so much more. You gave me a family, a safe place, the freedom to not look over my shoulder, and the best thing of all, knowing what unconditional love is. I love you."

"I love you too, baby." Blaze leans in for another kiss before the nurse takes the baby to weigh her, as another nurse comes in to check on Riley.

"Thank you for letting me be a part of the moment. I don't think I can ever express what it means to me," I tell them.

The nurse comes back and places the baby in Blaze's arms, and I grab pictures of Blaze with his little girl, who I know will be spoiled beyond belief.

I don't miss the moment Blaze looks over at Riley, and she gives him a nod.

"There was a reason we asked you two to be in here for the birth." Blaze pauses and smiles at Riley again. "Sage, you're my best friend, hands down. We have been through so much together. You said something to me that sent me to bed in tears that night. You said you thought the whole reason we went through everything we did with your birth parents was to be ready for Riley. When she showed up here, we knew how to help her. You said..." His voices cracks, and he squeezes his eyes shut.

Sage finishes the sentence, "I said that I finally understand why it happened to me. I was finally able to put it behind me and say that I'm glad it happened the way it did because I'd never seen you so happy, as you have been with Riley."

There's not a dry eye in the room at this point, me and the nurses included.

Then, Riley speaks, "And Lilly, that day you took a chance on me you saved my life, and I'm proud to call you my best friend. That day in your truck cab, I made myself a promise, and today, I get to keep that promise."

She squeezes Blaze's arm, and he walks over and places the baby in my arms. This sweet, little, pink skinned baby bundled up in a blanket. This sweet little girl doesn't flinch she just snuggles into me and continues to sleep.

When I look up, both Riley and Blaze are looking at me, and Blaze has his phone up taking pictures.

"We'd like to introduce you to our daughter, Lilly Sage Buchanan," Riley says. That's when I lose it, and thankfully, there's a couch behind me, as I sit down with this little baby that's the product of one split second decision that changed so many lives in one night.

When little Lilly grabs a hold of my finger, and my eyes meet Riley's, I completely lose it. My heart has never been so full. Knowing I will be here to see her grow up, to babysit, and to spoil her just makes this moment perfect.

I turn, seeing Sage and Blaze wrapped in a hug, both crying. When she turns to me, I place the baby in her arms and turn to Riley. Being careful, I wrap her in the biggest hug I can.

"I don't know what to say to this other than thank you. You're a sister to me, and you've given me more, much more than you can understand right now. So, thank you."

We spend a few more minutes with the baby before I turn to Blaze.

"Well, someone should go tell everyone the good news. If you want to stay with your family, I'm happy, too."

"Yes, go let them know and send Mom and Dad back."

I nod and give little Lilly a kiss, before stepping out into the hallway. I take a moment to get my emotions under control, but it's useless. I can't seem to get my eyes to quit leaking, as I head to the family waiting room.

I take one more deep breath, before walking through the doors.

Chapter 17

It's been a long morning here in the family waiting room. Since Lilly went back, I sent texts out to the ranch hands to make sure they knew what needed to be done today. We are expected to have more snow in a few days, so I want to make sure we are stocked up on what we need in the barn and to do a cattle check.

The bull that was caught in the fence is healing nicely, but I sent one of the guys to go check on him, before any more weather hits. Megan, Ella, and Sarah all fell asleep, waiting for their niece or nephew to be born. Ella's parents and her sister, Maggie, and brother, Royce, brought us all breakfast an hour ago, and things seemed to perk up a bit.

"So, Sage says you're looking to buy your own ranch in the area?" Colt asks me after we all get some food in our belly.

"Yeah, that was always the goal. I told Sage that when she hired me. I'm at a place where I can start looking now."

"The place next door to my parents went up for sale not too long ago. The family who owned it is really nice, but they're retiring down to Florida. I don't know much about it, but it might be worth a look," Hunter says.

"I hadn't heard, but thanks, I'll take a look," I tell him.

We talk a bit about different things to look for, and what I'd want in a ranch, but when we see Lilly step into the room with tears pouring down her eyes, the room goes still. I'm by her side before she can speak, pulling her into my arms.

"It's a girl," Lilly says, and the entire room erupts into cheers.

"They're both doing great. I've never seen anything like it in my whole life. Riley totally was meant to be a mom. Helen, Tim, they're asking for you."

Blaze's parents come up and hug Lilly. She gives them directions and a room number before I pull her back into my arms.

"Ella's parents brought breakfast. Are you hungry?" I ask her.

"Actually, will you go for a walk with me? I want to get some fresh air," Lilly asks.

"Of course," I say, following her out of the hospital and to the gardens on the side of the building.

As we enter the garden, I take her hand, and we walk along the pathways, soaking up the cold morning air.

"I know I said it before, but I've never seen anything like that in my life. I watched a ton of birthing shows to be ready for her, but nothing could have prepared me for the moment that little girl entered the world. There was a shift in the room. In the span of a minute, everything changed. Riley and Blaze became parents, and a new life entered the world."

"I'm so glad your truck needed to be worked on, so you could be here with her for the birth. I know it means everything to her."

"You'll never guess what they named their daughter," she says, as she stops in front of a bench across from a water feature. It's a peaceful place this early in the morning. I sit down and pull her into my lap, wrapping my arms around her.

"Please, tell me it's not something that will scar that poor child for life, like Gertrude or

Hilde."

She laughs, "No." Then, her face turns serious. "They named her Lilly Sage."

Wow. I always knew Lilly was special, and she means a lot to both the family and me. For them to name their daughter after her, is a huge thing, and now, I get why she was crying, when she walked into the waiting room.

"It doesn't surprise me. I know to Riley, you mean everything. When you aren't here, she's always talking about you. She worries about you being on the road, and she's always scheming for a way to get you to come visit and stay longer. It was her intention for you to fall in love with this place and move here."

"I know, and it's like it all sank in when I was holding that little girl. It's a huge ripple effect. I should have kept driving that night. When my mom heard I stopped to pick someone up at night, she laid into me something fierce. Just think though, how much different all our lives would have been if I hadn't stopped. I don't want to think about it, because I know this is where I'm meant to be, and where Riley is meant to be."

I hold her a little tighter, "I agree. You're meant to be here with them and with me. I feel it in my bones, Lilly."

I place my hand on the side of her face and turn her, so her eyes are on me.

"I know that night was meant not only to bring you here to them but to me, too."

"I agree. This feels like home." She leans in and kisses me. It's a light, sweet kiss, until she bites my bottom lip, causing me to groan.

I pull back and rest my forehead on hers for a minute, soaking her in. This all feels right, and I'm done fighting it. I want Lilly in my life any way I can have her, and now, I need to convince her that Rock Springs is where she needs to put down roots.

"Come on, let's head back in.

• • • • ● ● ● ● • •

Lilly

I try to gently get out of bed without waking Mike, but I should have known that wasn't going to happen.

"Go back to sleep, firecracker. The sun isn't even up yet."

I need to get out and meet the inspector at the ranch. He told me it was going to take half a day, so I booked it as early as he would let me. I also have a contractor meeting me on the site to get some estimates on work to be done. Plus, I can't tell Mike what I'm up to.

Lord forgive me for the lie I'm about to tell.

"I promised Riley I'd bring her breakfast, and I want some baby time before everyone else starts showing up today. And I need to get out and do some Christmas shopping."

I figure this way my bases are covered. I asked Riley to cover for me this morning, promising her all the dirt in a few days, and she agreed.

I try once again to get out of bed, but Mike flips me on top of him, pulling me down for a kiss. His hard length pressing against my belly makes me want him as badly as he wants me.

No matter the temperature, we both end up sleeping naked wrapped together. So, it's easy when Mike picks up my hips and slides inside of me before I can stop him. I groan and bury my head in his neck.

"Lilly." He gasps, as I start riding him, my hard nipples scrapping across his chest hair. The sensation is almost too much, as I sit up and rest my hand on his shoulder, staring down into his eyes.

He doesn't break eye contact, as we find a rhythm that has us both chasing our climaxes hard and fast. When he makes a small shift, I come, screaming his name, as he follows me over the edge.

"Mike," I groan, not moving. "That's one hell of a way to wake a girl up."

"Can't have you walking around out there in your sexy winter wear and not remind you whose you are."

"I know I'm yours. I couldn't forget."

"Good, then while you're out running around today, I want you to think about moving in here with me. No more sneaking out at night, and no more hiding."

My heart starts to race all over again, and it has nothing to do with the spectacular orgasm he gave me minutes ago. If I was ever worried about how he would react to the ranch, this moment shows he's ready to take this step with me, and I don't have to stop and think about it.

"Yes."

His eyes search my face before he breaks into a huge smile. "Yes?"

"Yes! I'll move my stuff in this afternoon, once I get back."

His face breaks out into a heart-stopping grin, but there's a mischievous twinkle in his eye as well. "Go get ready. Don't leave Riley waiting."

I rush into the main house, and I take a few minutes to pack some of my things, before grabbing the folder with all the ranch info I keep hidden in a jacket in the back of the closet.

I quickly make my way to Riley's truck. She said I could use it, and I make a note about getting one for myself. If everything goes well today, I might stop over at the car lot by the hospital and see what they have.

On the way over to the ranch, I go over in my head all the things I want the contractor to check. He also said he can look at the inspector's report and give me some quotes on what needs to be done.

As I pull into the ranch, Ryan is already there, and he greets me with coffee. "I also have some muffins inside that my mom made. She's testing out a new recipe and wants some unbiased opinions." He laughs.

We head inside, and the house is just as I remember it, except it's completely empty. It feels like home, even with all the work that needs to be done. Riley and Ella love to decorate, so I know they will want to help us, once renovations are complete.

I know Sage will have no problem with us staying at the ranch, while the work is being completed. From the way she and Blaze were talking, I'm sure they expect it, honestly. I know I will take some extra baby time wherever I can.

Another truck pulls up, and I turn to stare out the large, picture windows on the front of the house.

"Oh, that's Jimmy, the inspector. Have a muffin and meet us out in the barn, when you're ready." Ryan says as he heads out the door.

I grab a blueberry muffin, which is one of the best I've ever had, and then start walking the house, making notes for the contractor on things to fix, like updating the bathrooms and the kitchen. There are a few walls I'd like to see removed to make the space open, the carpets need to be removed, and smaller things like painting. I know we can do the painting in a weekend with help from everyone at the ranch.

I make my way out to the barn just as Ryan and Jimmy are coming out.

"The barn looks to be in good shape, Miss?" Jimmy says.

"Oh, you can call me Lilly."

"Miss Lilly. I would recommend a new roof sooner rather than later, and there are a few stalls that need to be fixed, but nothing you can't do on your own."

While he checks out the bunkhouses and foreman's house, I go into the barn and take a look. I will have to ask the contractor the best way to go about expanding it.

After we take in the bunkhouses and the foreman's house, all of which need a new roof and very little else, we make our way up to the main house, just as the contractor arrives.

"Wolf?" I ask him.

"Yes, you must be Lilly."

I nod, shaking hands with the large Native American Riley told me has done a lot of work for Blaze and Sage in the past.

"Blaze's wife told me you have worked with their family on many projects," I state.

"Yes! They're a great family and always good to our people. How are Riley and the little one? The Spirits told me the little one would be entering the world soon."

"She gave birth yesterday morning to a little baby girl, and they both are doing well."

"Oh, I will have to give her a call and give her my blessings. Now, show me around this beautiful land." He holds his hand out.

"Well, if we can keep this between us until Christmas, I would appreciate it. No one knows about this, because it's going to be a surprise. I'm going to settle down here in Rock Springs. It feels like home."

"It's calling to you. Many times, we don't pick where we live and settle. The land chooses us to watch over it in our lifetime and to be its keeper until we pass into the next life."

"I like that. I do feel a pull to this land that I can't explain any other way. I'd like to get quotes and some ideas on renovations to the main house, barn, and bunkhouses. The goal is to live here, but also take in and rescue horses, rehabilitate them, and use them during the summer for a kids' camp. We want to help kids going through difficult situations heal by connecting with the animals."

We head out towards the barn, and Wolf makes notes, as I look over at him, when a thought hits me.

"Wolf isn't your real name, is it? I know Mac's is Makya, but we all call him Mac."

"Yes, it's easier for those not from our tribe to have a simpler name. My name is Waya. It means wolf, so it's easier for outsiders to call me Wolf."

I nod, as we keep talking about changes here and there and go over the inspector's report, which showed nothing I wasn't prepared for.

"Let me review this tonight, and tomorrow, I'll email you separate bids for each building in case you chose to do them one at a time. I promise not a word until you say so."

"Thanks, Wolf."

Ryan locks up and meets me at my car. "The inspection went really well. Nothing major, Jimmy tells me. I'll have his full report in a few days, and then, we can move forward. We're still on track to close before Christmas."

Now to go look at a truck for me and make good on my promise to visit Riley.

Chapter 18

Riley is coming home from the hospital with baby in two days. The girls have been busy at the house, throwing a welcome to the world baby girl party, since they didn't get to do a baby shower.

I did my part and hung some decorations, and then I moved the rest of Lilly's stuff into my place. There wasn't much, as I had grabbed the important stuff yesterday when she was visiting Riley.

Now, I'm in the barn trying to stay out of the girls' way, when Hunter walks in.

"Hey, I took a look at that bull. He's all healed and a real pain in the rear end, too," Hunter says.

"Yeah, he's feisty alright," I tell him. "Hiding from the baby festivities?" I nod my head towards the house.

"Yeah. When it comes to all that, it's best to leave it to the girls."

"You're going to have one of those soon, you ready?"

"No, and yes. Thankfully, we're still five months away, but I'm ready to see Megan with the huge belly. I'm ready to play with my son or daughter, to hold him or her, and be a dad. But it's also scary that a little human will be dependent on me," he says, but I can see the twinkle in his eye.

"Well, the best part is you aren't alone. You have more people on this ranch to help out than I had family growing up. As long as you know when you need to ask for help, you'll rock the parenting thing."

"You too, you know? You have the support of everyone in there. You have always been more than just the ranch hand, and now with Lilly? You're one of us, family."

Do they really think of me as family? I know they consider me a friend, and I think of them as friends too, but family? I just shake my head.

"You don't think so? The day you buy your ranch you don't think every one of us will be there with boots on, prepared to work, and get it ready to go for you? If you don't, then you're a damn fool," Hunter puts his hand on my shoulder, before walking off.

His words are on my mind all day, as I prepare for my date with Lilly tonight. We got a fresh dusting of snow last night, and since they aren't doing the horse-drawn carriage rides at the winter festival this year, I thought tonight would be a good time to get one in.

After dinner, I ask Lilly to take a walk with me, and Sage hands me a thermos of hot chocolate I had asked her to prepare. We walk out the side door, and Lilly gasps.

A white sleigh with red seats and blankets sits in front of us with two large, white horses that Blaze had let me borrow for tonight. The sleigh is the church's, and with a donation, it's mine for the night.

"Mike! Did you do this?"

"I had a little help."

She leans up and kisses me on the cheek, before running over and petting the horses, and then climbing inside. We cuddle under the blankets, and I hand her the hot chocolate, as we head out down the driveway.

"I can't believe there's so much snow. Most years, there's no snow whatsoever," Lilly says in an amazed voice, staring around us.

"Yeah, it's perfect for Christmas. I think it was the universe forcing you to stay on the ranch, so you could fall in love with it."

She snuggles up to my side. "Well, the ranch isn't the only thing I fell in love with. I was already in love with the ranch, and I didn't need to be snowed in to know that."

I stop the horses and look over at her. She looks a little unsure, as a pink tint has covered her cheeks. I can't tell if it's from the cold or embarrassment from what she just admitted.

I lean over and kiss her ever so softly, feeling her melt back into me.

"I love you, Lilly. I think you being snowed in was just as much for me, as it was for you."

She takes a deep breath, running her eyes over my face. That feeling of warmth I get whenever her eyes are on me intensifies.

"I love you, Mike." She says barely above a whisper, before she leans in and kisses me hard, and with so much passion that when we pull back, we are both breathless.

I wrap her into my side and start the horses up again, as we talk about Riley and the baby. Before long, we round the corner, and the main house on the east side of the farm, where Tim and Helen live, comes into view.

It's all lit up, and the lights reflecting off the snow give a magical glow. We stop beside the porch, and Helen comes out with some of her cookies.

"Here are a few for you, and the rest go to Megan. She called me going on about craving cookies," Helen says.

"I promise to get the cookies to her," Lilly laughs.

We circle around and head back down the driveway and back towards the house, while we enjoy the cookies. As we come out of the tree clearing, the moment is just as I had hoped. The lights on the house and the barn are all lit up, and it has the same magical glow, as Tim and Helen's place. But it's even more spectacular because Sage spares no details on the decor. I stop the horses, and we sit there taking it in.

"It looks like it should be in some Christmas movie, where the big-time city boy falls for the small-time country girl."

"Our movie is the big-time city girl falls for the small-time country boy." I lean in to kiss her.

"Says the guy from Chicago," she murmurs against my lips, and I can't help but laugh.

"It's true, I am, but I think I was meant to be here. I couldn't move back to the city now, it's too noisy."

"Guess it's a good thing you have plans to own a ranch in small town USA then. It suits you." She finally steals a kiss, and her tongue dances across mine before she pulls back.

The lights hitting her face give off a soft glow, and it's then, I see light circles under her eyes. It hits me she has been more tired than normal too, barely keeping her eyes open, when her head hits the pillow.

"You okay, Lilly? You look exhausted."

"Yeah, just not used to the go, go, go of a large family." She looks over to the barn, shifting a bit in her seat.

I decide to drop it for now, but I'll keep an eye on her over the next few days.

"We better get Megan her cookies, or she's likely to kill us both," she says.

"Well, we can't have that." I laugh, as we head back to the house.

• • • • • • • • • •

This morning Lilly has a huge smile on her face, and it's not just from the orgasm I gave her, before we got out of bed, as much as I'd like to think it was.

"What's on your mind, Lilly?"

"I need you to give me a ride because I have a surprise."

I pour us both a cup of coffee and follow her out to my truck.

She tells me to head to the hospital, and she'll give me directions from there. I hold her hand the entire way, and it's comforting knowing she's next to me.

On the way, we talk about Riley and baby Lilly coming home tomorrow.

"They asked me to drive them home, and I'm so excited but really nervous. I know I've driven some valuable loads before, but there's nothing more precious than this little girl, and it's a long drive home."

"It's only twenty minutes." I remind her.

"It will feel like two hours, if I think about everything that could go wrong, flashing in front of my eyes."

She gives me a few more directions until we pull up to a car dealership.

She bounces out of the car before I can even ask what's going on. An older man greets her with a warm smile and a handshake, and I want to rip his hand off for daring to touch my Lilly.

Whoa. Where did that come from? I've never had possessive thoughts like that before, but there they are, front and center now. I make my way to Lilly's side and wrap my arm around her waist, watching the man's face. He makes eye contact with me and gives me a slight nod of understanding.

"What going on, firecracker?" I ask her, needing to understand.

"I'm here to pick up my truck."

"Your rig?"

"No, that's still in Amarillo." Something close to guilt crosses her face for a brief second before it's gone. So quick, that I'm sure I imagined it.

"I bought a truck to use when I'm here, so I don't have to keep borrowing everyone else's or asking for rides."

That's when I notice the keys in her hand.

"You know, I don't mind giving you a ride or letting you borrow my truck."

"I know, but I figure if I'm going to be in Rock Springs more, then I should have my own truck. I sold my car, when I left Tulsa because I had no need for it. Plus, it wouldn't have fit in on the ranch anyway."

She's thinking of putting down roots and staying in Rock Springs. The thought squeezes my chest and gives me hope.

"Well, show me this truck."

She walks a few spots down from where I parked.

"They call it firecracker red." She laughs.

"It's perfect for you." I take in the truck. It's a deep red and a few years old, but it looks to be in really good condition.

"You did good, Lilly. Let's head home. I'll follow you."

The whole way home, all I can think about is Lilly putting down roots, and what that will mean for us.

Chapter 19

"Isn't that so romantic?" Riley gushes after I finish telling her the story of the sleigh ride with Mike last night.

I glance at her in the review mirror. I'm driving her and Blaze home, so they can sit in the back with baby Lilly.

"Such good timing," Riley mumbles.

"Okay, enough of this. We have to get photos on the front porch with the snow in the background. Not only is it her first day home, but it's her first snow and first Christmas season."

This little girl is going to have the most magical birthday every year. I just hope she likes Christmas as much as her Aunt Sage does.

"I love it!" Riley agrees as we pull into the ranch. We head right to the front porch and get some photos. Baby Lilly gets passed around, and over a hundred photos are taken.

"That little girl is probably the warmest person here with the outfit, the blankets, and the body heat," I joke, as Mike walks up.

"And she's sleeping through it all. Lucky kid." He jokes.

The next few hours are the welcome home baby girl party with lots of cake, presents, and baby cuddles.

That night after dinner, I pull Mike to the side. "Can we stay in my old room tonight? I want to be close in case Riley needs anything," I ask him.

He kisses me on the cheek. "Of course. See you tonight."

I head upstairs to check on Riley and find her with Abby. Riley has chosen to breastfeed, and Abby is helping with latching, while also teaching her about pumping. Pretty much everyone in the house read up on it, once Riley announced she was going to breastfeed. She and Megan talked so much about it that Megan decided to do it, too.

Books were passed around, and there was at least one link a day in the group chat with info, ideas, and tips. It was then that I realized this family may be overwhelming to me at times, but they are so close and supportive. I'm lucky they have brought me into the fold, and again, I have Riley to thank for that.

I spend some time with them, before going to my old room and getting ready for bed. When my phone goes off, I have to stop myself from shouting. It's Ryan with the closing date I wanted. Everything went through, and I can't believe how everything lined up.

When my door opens, I barely get the phone turned off, before Mike's arms are around me.

"Come lay down with me. I need to hold you," he murmurs into my hair.

We lay down, and I turn to face him.

"Everything okay?"

"Yeah, I have you in my arms, so it's perfect now."

"What happened?"

"Ahhh, Hunter told me about the ranch next to his folks going up for sale, and I looked into it. Size wise it would have been perfect, but it's got a contract already. It went fast."

Guilt crashes over me. He's upset because of something I did. I should tell him, give up on the surprise, and just give him his gift early. I almost out myself then, but I have to remember this is a good surprise, and it will be worth it to wait to do this like I had planned.

I hope he sees it that way, and for the first time since I put this whole plan in motion, I start to doubt myself.

"I'm sure the perfect ranch is out there, and when it's the right time, you'll grab it, and I can't wait to be there when you do."

"Thanks, Lilly. Just holding you tonight, I'm already feeling so much better. I love you."

"I love you, too."

• • • • • • • • • • •

"I'm such a horrible person for keeping this secret from him. I should have told him, right? Of course, I should have. Is it too late? It's better to just wait it out now, right?"

I look down at baby Lilly in my arms. She was having problems sleeping after Riley fed her, so I got up and decided to walk with her a bit, so her mom and dad could sleep.

I wasn't sleeping anyway with the guilt of not telling Mike, eating at me. So much so, that I talked baby Lilly to sleep, too.

"I was wondering where you got off, too. I see I've been replaced," Mike jokes, as he joins me in one of the other guest rooms, where I have been pacing in front of the windows.

"She wouldn't sleep, and I couldn't sleep, so I figured no reason for everyone to be up." I sit down on the couch, and baby Lilly rests on my chest, falling right back asleep.

He doesn't take his eyes off me, as he sits beside me.

"Do you want kids?" He asks.

"Yeah, I hope to have a few kids someday. I'll probably get lots of practice in with this one." I kiss the top of her head.

"It's a sight to see you sitting there with the baby asleep on you. I want that with you, Lilly," he watches me.

Is this him telling me where he stands, and where we are? *This is big.* I feel it in my gut. We are living together, and I'm hoping everything is moving the direction I want with me buying this ranch.

Guilt grips me a little bit tighter, but when baby Lilly shifts and sighs in my arms, I remember it will all work out. It just has, too.

"I want this too with you. I've been thinking about it more and more since this little girl came home."

"Good, I'm glad we're on the same page," he says, resting his hand on the baby's back.

His hand is so large, and she is so small, that his hand covers her back from her neck to her butt. But there's something about it, seeing this huge, rough cowboy being so gentle with this small baby, that would make any girl's ovaries explode.

We sit there in the quiet for a bit, just watching her sleep, before Blaze comes in and finds us. "Hey, guess it's instinct that I woke up," he smiles, as baby Lilly starts moving around, giving a sign that she's hungry.

"Yep, you got the dad thing down," I tell him, as I give the baby a kiss on her head and hand her over to her dad.

"Get some sleep. Sage is up and wants to take the next shift," Blaze smiles.

"Sounds good. Don't be afraid to knock if you need anything."

Mike leads me back to bed, and this time in his arms, I'm asleep in minutes.

• • • • • • • • • •

I spent the morning helping Mike in the barn with the horses. I figure I need to start learning all I can, and I enjoyed working alongside him. I walk into the warm house, and Christmas music fills the air. I follow the sounds of laughter into the living room.

I find Blaze, Riley, and Sage huddled around baby Lilly, and Maggie standing over her with a camera.

"We're taking her first Christmas photos. I found so many cute ideas, and we're trying to see how many we can get done. Come see!" Riley waves me over.

"They're letting me get some practice in because I want to start doing photo shoots around here and make a business out of it," Maggie tells me.

As I get closer, I see baby Lilly sleeping in a red Christmas stocking surrounded by white Christmas lights. I have to admit these will be the most beautiful pictures. Maggie moves around getting pictures from all angles.

"Okay, let's put her in that sleeper, and then do the book one you showed me," Maggie says. She flips through the photos on the camera, showing me a few that are breathtakingly beautiful.

"You have a real talent, Maggie. Have you thought of taking ranch photos for businesses around here to use on their websites and advertising?" I ask her.

"Oh, I'd love, too!"

"Well, I know Mike is close to buying a ranch. I'd hire you to take before photos, so he has them after he fixes the place up," I say.

"Oh, that's a great idea, being able to put them side by side and see the old versus the new," Maggie nods. I sit on the couch and watch the photoshoot go on until Lilly starts crying and is ready to be fed.

"I guess, I need to talk to my parents about the photography," Maggie says, as she sits down beside me.

"You're talented and have a good eye. I bet people in town would love to go local for family photos and such."

"Yeah, I just hope it takes off soon. I want to prove I can stand on my own two feet." She says with a sigh.

"Prove to whom?" I ask.

The slight blush that covers her cheeks tells me it's a guy. The shake of her head tells me she doesn't want to talk about it, so I don't push.

Lying in bed that night with Mike, I finish telling him about the photo shoot, when he takes my hand.

"I want that with you, Lilly. The baby and a family. I loved working with you this morning, and I hope you'll want to do that when you're home from your truck runs. That's what I see when I see my future," he says, kissing my hand.

"I loved working with you this morning, too. If you had asked me a year ago where I saw myself, I didn't know, but I never would have thought of a ranch or even a small town. Now, I couldn't see myself anywhere else."

"Good, then my plan is working," he laughs, rolling over on top of me. "I mean it, Lilly. I love you, and I want you here with me."

I run both hands through his hair, pulling him closer to me. "There's no place else I'd rather be," I murmur, as I pull him in for a kiss.

He spends the night making love to me slow and sweet in such a way that our souls connect. It would crush me to let him go.

Chapter 20

Lilly, Abby, and Sage have been talking about the winter festival for days now, so we took a break from the ranch and decided to make an afternoon of it.

Abby has been pretty quiet, since she got here. She has spent some time with Sage, and she checks on Riley daily, but even Lilly mentioned the other day, she doesn't see much of her.

As we pull up to the church, it almost looks like the whole town is here. The church is built on land at the edge of town, and there's a huge empty space next to the building, where festivals like this fundraiser are held every year. The church holds at least five events, if not more each year.

"Oh, Sage. We have to try the food!" Abby takes her hand, and they head off in search of what treats Pastor Greg booked this year. He's always looking for fun food to draw in a crowd. I know WJ's has a booth here this year, and Nick is featuring some of his award-winning BBQ. That must be why it's so busy.

Before they get too far, we run into the sheriff.

"Sage and Mike, just who I need to talk, too." He nods his head off to the side, away from most of the people, and Lilly and Abby follow as well.

"We're working on tracking down an illegal rodeo that's happening around here. We aren't sure where, or who is involved, but it's been reported a few times. Horses have been stolen, and a few killed with signs of drugs and abuse that happen in these rodeos and illegal races. Please, keep extra security on your place. You're known to have good horses, and you'd be a target, if they get desperate enough. Also, please keep your ear to the ground on anything you might hear."

"Of course, Shane. Can you shoot me an email of things to look out for, if anyone brings a horse to me? I get people asking me to train horses for rodeo events all the time."

"Yes, I will. Though, I doubt they'd pay to have them trained properly. If you hear anything, even a slight bit of gossip you might think isn't helpful, please let me know."

"Make sure you talk to Jason, because he hears everything down at WJ's. Loose lips and all as people drink. Megan too with the church ladies at the salon." I tell the sheriff.

"I talked to him last night, and Megan is on my list today. I'm making the rounds, trying to get to everyone, reminding them to tighten up security. I know if someone tries to steal a horse out here, it won't be a pretty sight. These guys have high stakes and everything to lose by being caught."

"We'll let you know if we hear anything," Sage says before we say goodbye to the sheriff.

"I did some research on what happens at those rodeos, and it's not pretty. I hope they can put an end to this fast." Sage shakes her head, and then grabs Abby's hand. "How about that food?"

They walk off, following their noses to some of Nick's amazing BBQ.

I take Lilly's hand and start walking and taking everything in.

"What do you want to do first?" I ask her.

"I heard they set up an ice skating rink, so let's go find it," she starts pulling me along. Sure enough, to one side of the event, is a large ice skating rink lined with Christmas lights and a Christmas tree in the middle. There are speakers playing Christmas music, as everyone skates.

I get skates for us, and we slowly step out on the ice.

"Do I lose points if I fall? I haven't been ice skating in years," I tell her.

"Nope, as long I don't, because I haven't been skating, since I was a kid," Lilly laughs, holding my hand tight, as we slowly make our way around the rink. We have a few almost falls that have us laughing so hard that we can barely stand.

After the first round without any spills, we both loosen up. Lilly has a huge smile on her face and watching her light up, and the way the wind blows through her hair puts a smile on mine. She's so beautiful it hits you in the gut and doesn't let go.

I want more of this, and I just hope I can convince her to make Rock Springs home, once she gets back on the road. The thought of her leaving, even for work, doesn't sit well with me, but I won't stop her from doing something she loves. She has been so supportive of my dreams, and I want to make sure she can achieve hers, too.

We spend a while skating, and I love watching Lilly get brave and try a few spins. I stand there ready to catch her if needed, but she does great.

"You ready to go get some hot chocolate and warm up?" I ask her.

"Yes!"

We swap our skates out for our boots and head out in search of hot chocolate.

"Oh look, peppermint hot chocolate! Riley is going to be so sad. She's on a huge peppermint kick lately. Let's get some and go see the gingerbread competition," Lilly says.

"Sounds perfect."

Hot chocolate in hand, we go to the church event hall and check out all the gingerbread house submissions. The official judging is in a few days, but the town gets to cast their votes, too.

I was expecting that kids made the houses, but they're obviously done by adults. Some of these are pure works of art. There's a two-story one meant to look like a farmhouse with icicles, and it even has lights in it. Another used pretzels to make a small log cabin. One of my favorites used pecans as roof shingles and has a small fire pit in the yard.

We cast our votes and head out. "What next?" I ask her.

She's like a kid in a candy store so excited and full of life, as she pulls me towards some of the rides. At one point, my phone goes off.

"Hey, looks like Colt showed up, so Sage and Abby are going to go home with him," I tell Lilly.

"Good, let's check out the food next."

Pastor Greg did a great job with the food this year. He brought in classics like fried chicken, biscuits, and sweet tea. Then there's also a spot, which showcases Nick and his award from the Dallas BBQ competition. His booth is pretty busy, as he has a few new recipes up for everyone to try.

As we walk by, I hear a couple that just bit into their BBQ say the drive up from Austin was worth it for Nick's food. I smile and shake my head. That boy could work anywhere, and he chooses right here in Rock Springs. I'm learning that's the sign of a true country boy at heart.

Rock Springs has a way of getting its claws into your heart and pulling you in. Once there, you don't ever want to leave. Who would want to leave one of those classic small towns everyone wants to live in, but are so hard to find?

As we pass Nick's booth, we get to the classic carnival food. Fried Oreos, funnel cakes, walking tacos, and all things on a stick. Then there are the obscure foods like the fried Kit Kat bars, which neither of us could bring ourselves to try. I'm pretty sure all we could see is our lovely horse's face.

We did try the cookie fries, which are basically cookies that look like fries and are a bit lighter than actual cookies. We also had some Mexican corn, before we run into Sage, Abby, and Colt.

"Did you guys see the cookie fries?" Sage offers Lilly one.

"Yes, I don't think I could eat another bite," Lilly groans.

"You girls ready to head over to the tree lighting?" Colt asks.

"Oh, yes. We can't forget the tree lighting!" Sage loops one arm in Lilly's and one arm into Abby's, and they head off in front of me and Colt towards the large tree in front of the church. They had several men decorating it with the direction of the church ladies a few days ago. It was a sight to see, when I drove by the other day. They were all upset it was delayed, because of the snow.

"I love how the snow looks around the tree," Lilly sighs.

"Well, it's supposed to snow again this week, so there will be a fresh coat on the ground soon," I tell her.

We listen to Pastor Greg talk about the Rock Springs Christmas Tree tradition and a bit on the meaning of Christmas, and then he flips the switch. Not only does the tree light up, but so does the church.

The tree lights give off a magical glow, and so do the lights strung across the front of the church. It seems only right given the season.

"Let's get some hot apple cider and walk along Main Street enjoying the lights, before we head home," Sage suggests, and we agree.

Walking downtown with Lilly's hand in mine, as she talks and jokes with Sage and Abby, is the highlight of my night. It's such a simple moment that means more to me than she will ever know. I have found the town I want to be in, the community I want to be a part of, and the girl I want beside me. Now, I just need to find the land, which seems like an uphill battle.

Chapter 21

Mike

Today is the annual Christmas party at Tim and Helen's and pretty much the whole town shows up. Normally, I duck in, make a quick appearance, and then head out, claiming to check on animals for the night. If anyone asked, I'd say I wanted to get as much done tonight, so the others had a break tomorrow. With the day after tomorrow being Christmas Eve, no one ever made a big deal about it.

This year everything is different. I will have Lilly by my side, and I plan to stay as long as she wants. The girls are getting ready in Sage's room, and Blaze invited me to get ready with him and the guys at the other end of the house in one of the guest rooms.

"So, any plans on when you are popping the question?" Blaze asks, and all eyes go on me.

How did he know? I haven't told anyone I was thinking of asking Lilly to marry me. I haven't even really admitted it to myself that I wanted to.

"Don't worry, I can see the panic in your eyes. I've been watching you two, and it's the look. I know if you aren't there yet, you will be soon." Blaze answers my silent question.

I let out a sigh of relief, speaking my thoughts for the first time.

"I was thinking for Christmas. Is that too cheesy?"

"No, girls love that kind of thing," Colt says.

"But Lilly isn't any girl, and I want her to love it," I tell them.

The room is quiet, before Hunter speaks, "Maybe, think of something special to her and incorporate that. I proposed in the field that holds a lot of memories for Megan and me."

"I proposed in the barn I first saw Riley in," Blaze adds.

"I proposed at the lake house just a few steps from where I was, when I saw Sarah for the first time," Mac says with a goofy smile on his face.

"I proposed at Megan's wedding reception because I first saw Ella in the same place at Sage's wedding reception," Jason says.

I look over at Colt, and he smiles and shakes his head. "I sent Sage on a scavenger hunt all over the ranch and town, but I proposed in our cabin, the one that holds the best memories for us."

"Where was the first place you saw Lilly?" Blaze asks.

"In the barn, she was taking a breather and watching the cows in the pasture," I tell him.

"Where did you first say I love you?" Colt asks.

"In the sleigh ride in front on the driveway right out there," I point towards the front of the house.

"Just a few ideas," Hunter shrugs. "You know her best, don't overthink it, and we're here to run ideas by."

"You know, Riley would love to help you plan something, right?" Blaze asks.

"Yeah, I've been thinking of it, but I want to do this myself."

The guys all nod and agree, and then thankfully, they change the topic, as we finish getting ready and head downstairs to wait for the girls.

Lilly is one of the last ones to come downstairs, and she takes my breath away. All I can see is her in the dark, red, lace dress and cowboy boots. Her hair is down in loose waves, and the turquoise jewelry she has on makes her eyes pop.

I finally regain the use of my legs and meet her at the bottom of the stairs.

"You look stunning," I say, my voice a bit hoarser than I intended.

She runs her hands down the front of my button-up shirt. "You look pretty damn good yourself there, cowboy."

When we walk into the party, I feel everyone taking her in. Lilly isn't one to dress up, but I know after tonight, I will be finding more ways to get her to dress up because she's the most beautiful girl I've ever seen.

She's beautiful in jeans and a t-shirt or flannel, but she's drop dead gorgeous in a dress with her hair all done up.

The first person to greet us, when we walk in is Brice. He runs the doctor's office in town with his dad. He and Sage dated for a bit, parting as friends before Colt stepped up his game.

"Hey, Mike. I tried those vitamins you recommended on my mom's horse, and they are amazing. She has so much more energy, which makes my mom happy. Thank you," Brice says.

"Hey, you're welcome. Hunter was the one who told me about them, so I can't take all the credit. Horses are a lot like us. The older we get we need a bit of a boost, only coffee isn't a good idea for horses," I laugh.

We chat for a minute more, before heading in. Royce leads Anna Mae to the dance floor, and I turn to Lilly. "May I have the honor of this dance?" I ask her.

"Of course," She smiles, taking my hand.

We dance through a few songs, before taking a break. "You thirsty?" I ask her.

She nods, so I get some water and find Maggie and Nick in the kitchen. Nick is cooking the food tonight, and Maggie is taking photos for Jason to use on the website and social media to promote his food.

"Hey, how's it coming?" I ask.

"She's taking pictures of every little thing from twenty different angles," Nick acts like he's annoyed, but there's a glint in his eye.

"Well, I haven't worked with food before, so I want to make sure there's something usable from this batch," Maggie says.

"Maggie, I've seen your stuff, and it's amazing. There will be more photos than we'll know what do with," Nicks says.

There's something there I feel it, so I back out of the kitchen to let them have their moment and go to search out Lilly. I find her, standing with Abby and Pastor Greg, and she's holding baby Lilly while talking with them.

The sight is one I don't want to forget. The Christmas decorations all over and the lights glittering around her. The baby asleep in her arms, and she has a huge smile across her face, as she talks with Abby. She's at ease, lightly rocking the baby in her arms.

A vice grips my heart, and my future is instantly crystal clear. I want Lilly as my wife. I want many more Christmas's like this one. Soon, I want it to be our baby in her arms. I carefully slip my phone out of my pocket and take a picture to capture this moment. I know it's one I will want to look back on.

Like she can sense me looking at her, her eyes meet mine, and she excuses herself from the conversations to come join me.

"You could have come over and joined us," she says.

"I was taking it all in. You look so beautiful and happy, and I wanted to memorize the moment," I tell her.

She looks down at the sleeping baby in her arms, and then back up at me.

"I want to give you your Christmas gift tomorrow, just the two of us. Can you get away for a bit?"

"Of course, I can. Can I have a hint what it is?"

She acts like she's thinking by pursing her lips together and trying to fight the smile on her face.

"Well, it's not on the ranch. We have to head towards town, and that's the only hint you get."

"Why don't you go back and join them? I need to talk to Riley about something before I forget."

I kiss her temple and watch her walk back over to Abby and Greg, picking right back up in their conversation. I find Riley on the back porch cuddled up with Blaze, drinking some hot chocolate.

"I'm sorry to interrupt, but I need to ask a favor of Riley," I say. Her eyes sparkle, almost like she knows exactly what I'm about to ask.

"Anything." She says without hesitation.

"You don't by chance have a way to get a hold of Lilly's parents, do you?"

"No, but I have her sister's number, and she's spending the holiday with her parents."

"Could I get it from you?"

She stares at me for a moment in silence. "I'm not in the habit of giving out someone's number without their permission without a good reason."

I take a deep breath and look at Blaze, who has a slight smile on his face.

"I want to ask Lilly to marry me, but I have yet to be able to talk to her dad. I was hoping to maybe set up a video call because I'd like to propose very soon."

Riley lets out a squeal and then pulls out her phone. A moment later, I feel mine go off.

"I won't say a thing. Go down to the end of the porch there. The double doors are Tim's study. They should be open, make your calls in there. I'll let Tim know you're in there, he won't mind."

"Thanks. And Riley, not a word."

"I promise, now go!"

I head down to the end of the porch, and just like she promised, the door is open. I duck inside and turn on a light. Sitting on the couch, I call the number she gave me.

"Hello?" A hesitant voice answers.

"Hello, Savannah. This is Mike from..." I don't even get a chance to finish my sentence.

"Mike! Is Lilly okay?"

"Yes, I'm sorry to bother you, but Riley gave me your number. I was wondering if there was any chance I could get on a video call with your father?"

The line is silent. I have to pull the phone away from my ear to make sure the connection is still there.

"Is there any particular reason?"

"Yes, but I'd like to talk about it with your father."

"Okay, let me call you right back." Then, the line goes dead.

I sit there in the quiet and try to think of what I want to say, and how I plan to convince him from miles away that I'm the one for his little girl.

The phone rings again from Savannah with a video call. I answer, and a man who I assume is Lilly's father is front and center. Lilly's sister is behind him to one side, and an older woman I think is her mother is by Savannah on the other side.

"Mike, this is our father and my mother." Savannah motions to each one.

"Hello, Mike! Lilly has told us so much about you." Lilly's mother gushes. "You can call me Cammi, and this is my husband, Allen."

"You can call me Allen, only because Savannah has too many nice things to say about you," Allen says no emotion on his face. I have a feeling he knows where this conversation is going.

"I know it's the holidays, so I'll keep this short. I was hoping to meet you in person, but this snowstorm threw us all for a loop."

"I heard about that. How is everyone doing there with the snow?" Allen asks.

"The ranch seems to be holding up well. Every time we get the roads cleared it seems more snow falls, but it hasn't been too bad. Just slows down the work, but it's nothing we can't handle."

He nods his head and then cuts right to the point. "Well, let's hear it." He says.

I smile just a bit. He reminds me of my dad, who is not one to dance around the subject. I know my dad likes it, when others don't as well, so I decide to go right to the point.

"I love your daughter, sir. I'd like to ask your permission to marry her. I know right now I'm just a ranch hand with little to offer, but I've been saving for years to buy a ranch, and the only thing stopping me is finding the right property."

"Savannah told me of your plans to rescue horses and run a summer camp for kids." Allen states.

I nod my head. "Yes, depending on the land I get. It would determine the fall and winter activities as well. I plan to make the ranch self-sufficient with meat and produce, and I'll make sure there's a place for Lilly's rig. I won't ever ask her to give up trucking, as long as it's what she wants to do."

"How do you plan to take care of her until then?" He asks me.

"Well, we'll stay here, and I'll keep working for Sage on the ranch. Everyone knows I'm looking for a ranch and have been really helpful. They said I can stay as long as I need, even after I buy the land, so I can do any renovations. I have my own cabin on the ranch, so we would have our own space."

"Tell me a bit about your family. I know what Lilly has said, but I want to hear it from you," Allen says again with no emotion on his face.

"Yes, sir. I'm an only child. Grew up in Chicago. My dad owns a very successful business there, and my mom was what you would call a society lady, but she wasn't one of those mean stuck up ones. She only worked with charities and causes she believed in, and she was also a stay at home mom for me. I rarely had a babysitter, and she was always at every school event, PTO meeting, and field trip. My dad was the kind to drop everything to be at one of my events. When I was about thirteen, a rodeo came to town, and we went as a family. I knew then I wanted to be a cowboy, and I told my parents." I pause, lost in the memory, before continuing.

"They supported me 100% and made me a deal. If I went to school to get a ranch management degree and work for five years on a ranch to learn the business while I saved money, they would help me get my ranch. The deal right now stands. He'll buy my first round of horses and pay for their upkeep for a year since I have met their terms."

I stop, realizing I've been rambling, and no one has said a word.

"What if Lilly doesn't want to work on the ranch?" Allen asks.

"Well, the land will be big enough for her to do as she likes. If she wants to open up a shop like you did, I'd make it happen. I don't see her having much interest in opening a store in town, but I'd support her if she wanted to do that, too."

Allen finally moves and turns to look at his wife. I think he put me on mute, because I hear nothing from their end, as the three of them talk. After a few minutes, he turns back to me.

"We give you our permission, but I expect to meet you in person before we're in town for the wedding. Do you hear me?" Even though his voice is stern, I can't help the big smile on my face.

"Yes, sir. After all this snow clears, I'll make it happen."

We exchange phone numbers, before ending the call.

I let out a sigh of relief, before heading back to find my girl.

Chapter 22

Lilly

I have been up since sunrise. I'm so nervous because today is the day I take Mike to the ranch. Today is the day I admit what I have been hiding from him. Today is also the day I admit that I quit trucking. I'll tell him that, when he took me to Amarillo, I was turning in my rig. I know he will love this ranch, and now, we'll be able to start the life together we've been talking about.

I start getting ready when Savannah texts me.

Vanna: Call me soon as you can. I want to know how he took it! I'm so excited for you two!

Me: Promise!

After breakfast, Mike looks at me, "So, is it too early to ask about my gift?" He rocks on his heels. He's like a kid in a candy store who's allowed to spend a lot of money, as his grin spreads across his face.

"Nope, let's go. Grab your jacket," I tell him and get my keys. He doesn't even fight me and lets me drive.

"If I guess, will you tell me?" He asks once we are heading towards town.

"Sure, but I doubt you will," I say, taking a quick glance at him. He starts to name different ideas from food to people visiting. None are even remotely close, but I file away ideas for later use.

I turn down the road that leads to Hunter's parents' house.

"Oh, did you get Hunter's mom to make me her wings? Oh man, she makes the best wings in the world," Mike rests his head back on the headrest, and then rolls his head to look at me.

I laugh, "No I didn't. It has nothing to do with food."

I pull down the drive to the ranch next door to Hunter's parents.

"What are we doing here? This place sold fast." He's sober, as he looks around. I drive up to the main house and get out.

He follows me, looking hesitantly around.

"Are we allowed to be here?" He asks.

"Yep. I know the owner. What do you think of this place?"

"It's beautiful."

I take his hand, "Come on, let's check out the outbuildings."

We walk slowly towards the barn in silence, enjoying the early morning Texas air, and the little snow on the ground. This is the first time I've been here since I signed the papers and closed on the property two days ago.

He watches, as I unlock the barn with the key I have, but he doesn't ask any questions. I pull open the tall double doors and let light into the barn. It's fairly clean right now with no animals here, but it's well taken care of, and Mike takes it all in.

"There's more than enough room here, and it's in great condition," he says, looking around.

I take his hand and lead him towards the back door, where you can see the pasture and horse training rings.

"They used that section over there as an obstacle course. The jumps and all are in the storage shed. There are barrels for barrel racing, too," I tell him.

He takes it all in quietly with little emotion on his face.

I close up the barn and head towards the bunkhouses.

"There are two bunkhouses, and it's great because there could be a boy's and a girl's bunk. Then, the foreman's house is over there. It's a large three bedroom, but it would make a great space for counselors with a little renovation."

He has a faraway stare in his eyes, and I have to wonder if he's picturing what it could be like just as I did that first day here. He opens his mouth to talk, but I cut him off, worried he's going to want to leave before I finish the tour.

"Come on, let's go look at the main house." We walk in silence back up to the main house. He keeps his hands in his pockets and seems very careful not to touch me.

I open the front door, and we walk in, and he takes a look around, and then stops in the middle of the room, looking back at me.

"Why are we here, Lilly?"

"There's a creek that runs along the back of the property as well as horse trails to it. Hunter's parents have a small lake on their property, and they have agreed to let us use it with the kids or just for ourselves if we put a gate in the fence. It's perfect for picnics."

"Lilly, this ranch sold."

"Yes..." I pause and take a breath. I hear my sister in my head, screaming just say it like she did when we were little. "...to me."

He jerks his head back to look at me, but there isn't a hint of emotion on his face. So, I fill in the blanks.

"When we went to Amarillo, it wasn't because my truck was going to be worked on. I turned it in. I quit and picked up my last paycheck. When Savannah was here, this place was up for sale, and I was talking about how perfect it was for you, and she wanted to help, so we bought it. For you." I trail off at the end.

He doesn't say anything, just looks around, so I continue with a need to fill the silence.

"I stopped here the day I heard it was for sale. I didn't want to mention it to you until I knew if it was a fit or not. I walked in here, and I saw us eating dinner at the table and watching TV at night. I saw us working in the barn, and our kids running around, and I knew this was the dream I wanted, too. For the first time, getting back on the road, filled me with dread. That's when I knew I was done trucking because I was more excited about starting this dream than I was upset about giving up that one."

"You bought this place?" He finally looks at me.

"Well, yes with Savannah's help I bought it for you."

He starts shaking his head, and then it's like a switch flipped. "No, this is too much. You bulldozed in and didn't include me. You've been lying to me. It's not what was supposed to happen. I worked my butt off to buy the ranch. Me." He walks out of the door, leaving me stunned and feeling like I was slapped across the face.

I thought he'd be happy. In all the times I pictured this moment, I never thought it would go like this. This place is perfect. Hunter's parents and a vet live next door. I can't even move to go after him, even though I know I should.

I don't even realize I'm crying until the tears are running down my cheek. I can't remember the last time I cried. I trained myself not to show emotion on the road. I wipe them away and leave. I can see Mike walking towards Hunter's parents' house, so I get in the truck and head after him.

"Get in the truck. I'll take you home," I say, rolling down the window.

"Go home, Lilly. I called for a ride."

"Damnit, Mike. Just get in the truck."

"I'm fine. I need time to think anyway."

That's guy code for I need to figure out how to break up with you. I roll up the window and head back to the ranch in shock. I don't remember a thing about the drive there, but suddenly, the ranch is in front of me. I park the truck, leaving the keys in the ignition and head right to my room.

Sage and Ella both try to talk to me as I walk in, but I don't hear them. I just go to my old room, lock the door, and let it all out. I fling myself on the bed and cry. How was I so stupid? I really thought he'd be happy and want to jump into planning our life together. How could I have been so wrong?

I reach for my phone and call Savannah.

"Lilly! How did it go?"

"Not good."

"Oh, God! Lilly, you're crying! What happened? Tell me."

I explain the whole morning to her, how I surprised him, and his reaction down to him walking off and not coming home with me.

"Oh, Lilly. No one would have thought he'd act that way. I thought he'd be as excited as you. If the situation was reversed, I know you'd be over the moon. I'm the last one to ask about boy advice. Want me to call Mom in and tell her what happened? She was always the best at this."

"Yeah," I sniffle.

I hear a muffled Savannah explaining to my mom what I told her, and then I hear Mom's voice.

"Lilly, baby? I put you on speakerphone. Vanna is still here, too."

"Hi, Mom."

"You might not like what I have to say, but I think this is a guy thing. He's old fashioned and wants to be the one to take care of you and not the other way around. He's been working for this dream for what did you say, five or six years now? I'm sure he'd dreamed of buying the ranch, picking it, making an offer, signing the papers, and with this, it's just gone. Give him time. If he truly is the one, he'll see what a blessing this is to start a family and a life together."

"I didn't think of it like that," I wipe my tears.

"I know, baby. You have such a good heart, and you wanted to surprise him. If he knows you, he'll see that I promise. Now, go snuggle that little baby and give her a kiss from me. It will make you feel better." Mom pauses, before she speaks again, "Lilly, do you plan to keep the ranch, even if he doesn't come around?"

"Yes. I'm sure Sage can give me a crash course on everything I need to know. Worst case, I guess I can lease the land and live in the house. I'm going to take a few days, and then start looking into it."

"Okay, baby. Go get some snuggles. Everything will look better tomorrow, you'll see."

"Thank you, Mom. I love you."

"I love you too, Lilly."

"Love too, Vanna."

"Love you, Lilly. I'm a call away anytime you want to talk."

I hang up the phone and lay there, replaying the morning in my head, until I hear a knock on the door. Hoping it might be Mike here to talk, I run to the door, but find Riley on the other side.

"I'm guessing I'm not who you were hoping to see?"

I just shake my head and lay back on the bed. Riley lies beside me and pulls me into her arms, and I spill it all over again and cry myself to sleep.

Chapter 23

Mike

I'm sitting on Hunter's parents' front porch, waiting for Colt to come pick me up. Part of me wants to text Lilly and make sure she made it back to the ranch okay, since it just started to snow again, and another part of me is so angry, I know I shouldn't.

I still can't wrap my head around what just happened. She bought an entire ranch as a Christmas gift for me. Did she think I couldn't do it on my own? That I'd never get there because it's been a year?

I was being picky, and it wasn't because I couldn't do it on my own. It's because this is the place I plan to spend the rest of my life and be able to pass down to my kids. If we are lucky, they will pass it down to their kids.

I look over towards the ranch. It's perfect. It's everything I've been waiting on, and you can't get much better neighbors than Hunter's parents and a vet to boot.

I never thought Christmas Eve would be spent fighting with Lilly. I shove my hands into my pockets, feeling the ring there. The one my mom gave to me when they were here visiting for Thanksgiving. It's my grandmother's wedding set. She knew then just by the way I talked about Lilly that she was it for me. She knew before I did.

Lilly's face flashes in my mind. How excited she was to show me the ranch, and the hurt in her eyes, as I walked out of the door. I throw my hat on the ground, "Damnit."

"Now, what did that hat ever do to you?" Colt asks as I glare over at him. I hadn't heard him pull in. I pick up the hat and take a deep breath. None of this is Colt's fault, and I won't be the asshole who takes it out on him either.

"Let's head home, and I'll tell you all about it," I tell him.

"Sounds good."

On the way back to the ranch, I tell him everything that happened this morning. From me sending Lilly home on her own, and why I'm sitting on Hunter's parents' porch.

Colt is quiet and listens to it all.

"What is it that you're really upset about?" He asks.

"What? Did you not hear me?"

"I heard you. What I heard was the girl you love and planned to ask to marry you just quit her job, because she wants to work beside you. She bought your dream ranch for you two to start your lives together. She gave you the perfect opportunity to drop on your knee and ask her to marry you, and you walked out the door pissed off at her. Then, you let her drive back to the ranch in this weather alone. So again, what part are you mad about?"

"I've been working towards this for six years, saving and learning. I was dreaming of closing day, and I didn't get that, because she took it from me."

Damn, that thought hadn't crossed my mind the whole time I was stewing on the porch. But when Colt asked, it was there and out of my mouth, before I could think twice.

"I hear you. Maybe, you are looking at it wrong."

"How else is there to look at it?"

"Do you know how stressful it is to buy a ranch? Especially, in such a short amount of time? Sage, me, and the family we have been through it, buying Sage's family's land. The inspections on every building, the property lines, the surveyors, and the soil tests. She took on all that stress and handed you your dream, asking to be part of it."

I look out of the window. I knew the process of buying land out here. I've researched it, and he's right, the inspections alone on the buildings could have been overwhelming.

I think to my time with Lilly these last two months, and there were days she seemed more tired than others, and I wrote it off as helping with the baby, Riley, or the ranch. Was it really everything she was doing for our ranch?

My heart skips a beat when I think of it as our ranch. *Our home.* Did she say she saw our kids running around in the house? Damnit.

"You don't think this was too much?" I ask Colt.

"Let me ask you this. If she came to you and said she was thinking of giving up trucking to work on the ranch with you, what would you have said?"

"I wouldn't have let her, because trucking was her dream. She loves it and is damn good at it."

"Do you want her gone for a week or more at a time?"

"No, I want her home of course, but she..."

"She gave up one dream for the one she wanted more, Mike. She made that choice. This was her way of showing you she was all in and not going to pack up and leave the first chance she got. What did you do the first chance you got to prove you were all in?"

"You're on her side?"

"I'm on my wife's side, who is going to side with Riley, who will side with Lilly, which means Blaze will be coming to you for answers. That girl doesn't trust easily, and it sounds like the first sign she gave you of that trust, you threw it in her face. So, the only question that matters is do you love her?"

"Of course, I love her."

"Then does it matter who bought the ranch, if at the end of the day you are both sleeping on that land in each other arms for the rest of your life? Or is it more important for you to go through the stress of buying a property and sleeping on the land alone every night? Coming from someone who made the wrong choice and slept alone for years, I can tell you there's nothing worth that kind of pain, but that's just me."

I try to picture running a ranch without Lilly by my side, and the thought makes me sick to my stomach. I don't know when it happened, but at some point over the last several weeks, my dream has transformed from me running the ranch to us running the ranch, and I don't think I want to do it alone anymore.

We pull into the ranch, and Colt puts the truck in park, before turning to look at me.

"Listen, you have the day to think about it. Make sure the choice you make is the one you can live with for the rest of your life because you're the one who has to live with it. There's no guarantee you'll get the chance to change your mind."

I watch him head inside, and then look over at the cabin. Is she in there? Is she waiting for me? Hope fills my heart until I get inside and find it empty. Her stuff is still right where we left it this morning, so my guess is she hasn't been here.

I leave the door unlocked, even though I doubt Lilly will be back tonight. She's probably back in her old room at the main house. I lie on our bed and take a deep breath, letting her scent surround me. I pull out the ring I've been carrying around with me.

I love Lilly with my whole heart. I don't doubt that for a second. I don't want to picture my life without her. I snapped because I wasn't a part of the process. I wasn't there to sign the papers, and I didn't get a say.

I had been dreaming of closing day for years. Holding the keys in my hand and walking onto the land for the first time.

I wanted to carry Lilly over the threshold the first time we walked into the house together.

Colt is right, though. She took on the stress to do this for me. This was her way of proving she was all in, and I stomped all over it. Shit, did she even make it home okay? I shoot off a text to Blaze to ask.

Blaze: Maybe, you should ask her.

Me: Listen, I know I screwed up okay. Just let me know she's okay, so I can stop worrying and work on my plan to get her back.

Those three little dots indicating he's typing show up and disappear four times before a text comes in.

Blaze: She's here and safe.

Me: Thank you. I promise, I'm going to make this right.

Blaze: You better. The girls aren't very happy with you.

Me: Can't blame them.

I toss my phone on the bed beside me. I think about the property. It's perfect, and there would be a few adjustments needed to get it going by summertime, but I think we could do it.

Is my old dream of signing papers and doing inspections worth losing my dream of Lilly as my wife and my future with her? Trying to picture running the place without Lilly, makes my heart feel like it's being sliced open.

My dream has shifted. I want Lilly in it, and having her, is more important than the papers and inspections. I've gotten used to her here in the cabin and in my arms every night. There's nothing worth giving that up for.

Knowing she's safe and in good company, I take the night to get my head on straight and make my plans to win her back.

Chapter 24

Lilly

I couldn't sleep last night, so I got up and went for a walk at sunrise. I know once the house comes alive for the Christmas Eve festivities, it won't stop until everyone is in bed tomorrow after Christmas day.

There's something so peaceful about the ranch at sunrise. I walk down the driveway behind the house to the closest fields. The snow crunches under my boots and the fog of my breath fills the air in front of me, as yesterday's events fill my mind once again.

I still haven't heard from Mike. Colt did mention he picked him up and brought him home, so I know he's here, which is part of the reason I snuck out of the house, like a teenager. At some point, I will have to go get my things from the cabin, but I just don't think I'm ready to face him yet.

I'm pretty sure I could ask Riley, and she'd be happy to do it. Although, that's the least of my problems. I have several hundred acres I need to figure out what to do with now. Vanna said she will support whatever choice I make, but that I should wait, until after the first of the year to make any big decisions.

If Mike and I can't work this out, I'd want to just give him the property, but I know he won't take it. He made that perfectly clear. So now the question is, what to do with it, and do I still plan to stay in Rock Springs?

I don't even have to think about it. I know I want to be in Rock Springs, even if Mike and I don't work out. It will hurt to see him with someone else one day, but this is my home, and he isn't going to change that. I decided a long time ago this was home, and I think I started putting down roots before I even realized I did.

I love the property, and while I'm in no position to run a ranch, I do want to live in the house and remodel it. I got the estimate from Wolf, and I can do the house first. The cost came in less than I had planned for the main house.

I can rent out the land. I know several ranchers in the area are looking to rent land to hold their cattle on or to use to make hay. Sage can teach me what I need to know about horses, and I can board horses in the barn. That should be enough to cover the ranch costs until I figure out what to do. Even if I just remodel it, then sell it to buy something more manageable down the road.

Another option is to rent the house out as well, after doing a bit of work on it. This is an option I have been leaning towards, because every time I pictured living there, it was with Mike and building a family with him. I don't know if I can see myself living there alone.

As I walk through a clearing, I stop and take it all in. I'm starting to understand Sage's love for this land. To see what your hard work can do. I haven't been here as long as she has, but I already have some of my own memories here, and I know of many of hers.

It's at that moment I know I want to keep the ranch. I want to be here and own the land. Someday, I will have kids to pass it down to, and that thought excites me. Just as quickly, the balloon pops with the voice in the back of my head, saying it won't be with Mike.

I cried so much last night that I'm thankful I don't seem to have anything left in me to cry.

I walk over to a fallen tree, brush off the snow, and sit down. I close my eyes and listen. Everything is so quiet. A little rustling of leaves in the trees behind me and the sounds of the cows in the next pasture.

I check my phone and shoot up a prayer of thanks that I have service here, and I call my sister. I know it's early, and she will still be sleeping. She will probably cuss me out, but I want to talk to her now.

"You better be dying." Savannah's groggy morning voice greets me, as I suspected it would.

"No, I've been up for a bit thinking."

I hear some movements on her end and assume she's sitting up in bed, trying to clear her head.

"You promised no big decisions, until after New Year's." Savannah ends on a yawn.

"I know, and I won't, but I've been thinking of my options."

"And what did you come up with?"

"I want to stay in Rock Springs. I always pictured Mike and I running that land together. It's hard to change that dream, but I think I want to keep the land. I want to live there and work it. I want to pass it down to my kids."

"How are you going to make it work because if I know you, there's a plan in place already?"

"At first, I can rent out the land, until I'm ready to work it. I was thinking of fixing up the barn and boarding horses. Many of the corporate people in Dallas like to board a horse for weekends or for their kids. I can set up a few trails down to the creek. I'll renovate the main house, and if living there is too much, I can always rent it out or resell, once I fix things up. At the very least, I can look at it as an investment property, and at most, it will be my home. Only time will tell."

"Well, you know I'll support whatever you want to, as will Mom and Dad." She yawns again, which brings a smile to my face. "What are your plans for today?"

"Lots of baking. I might go over to Tim and Helen's to help her with the pies and cookies."

"And to avoid Mike."

"Yeah, I just need space right now. I have no idea what to say to him. You know, I still have to go to the cabin and get my stuff. I know I need to be an adult and do it right."

"But?"

"But I want to get Riley to get Blaze to keep him busy and sneak in to do it, so I don't have to face him. I'm just not ready, but I need clothes!"

This causes Vanna to laugh. "What're you wearing now?"

"Thankfully, Riley is my size. Well, she says she was before her pregnancy, so she let me borrow some clothes. I'm not going to lie, her maternity clothes looked pretty damn comfortable. I'm kind of jealous."

"As much as I'd love a niece or nephew, don't go getting any ideas right now. I have a tour coming up, and I want to be there during your pregnancy."

"I have to find a man first, Vanna."

The sound of crunching snow catches my attention. It's still early, so I guess someone else is out for a walk as well.

"Hey, I need to get going, but I'll call later to talk to Mom and Dad, okay?"

"Okay, love you, Lilly."

"Love you too, Savannah. And thank you."

I put my phone in my pocket and take one last look at the quiet field, before turning to greet whoever is about to break through the clearing.

I was expecting one of the ranch hands, or even Riley coming to find me. I didn't expect to see Mike standing there.

He looks like he didn't sleep much either last night. He keeps his eyes on me, but neither of us says a word. The tension is high, and I finally just can't take it anymore.

"I was just heading back in. It's all yours," I tell him, as I go to walk past him to the trail that leads back to the house. I hear a sharp intake of breath, as I walk by, but I don't stop.

"I actually came out here to see you."

That stops me in my tracks, as I turn to see him watching me.

"I saw you come out this way. I waited to catch you on your way back, but I got impatient." He shoves his hands into his jacket pockets and looks down at his feet.

"What do you want?" I get straight to the point, but what I want is to go inside and warm up, and honestly, just get Christmas over with, so I don't have to paste on a fake smile.

Maybe, I'll go spend a few weeks with my parents, until New Year's just to get a break and some distance from this place, if I can't even go twenty-four hours without running into Mike.

"I'm sorry about yesterday. This picture I had in my head of buying a ranch blinded me. I didn't want anything different."

I don't know what to say, because I don't know where he's going with this.

"Will you go for a drive with me?" He asks, his expression unsure.

My knee jerk reaction is to say no, turn around, and walk away. But my heart is telling me this might be my only chance to mend this. As much as yesterday hurt, I still picture him by my side, and I don't think I'm ready to give up on that just yet.

Not trusting my voice, I just nod then turn and head back to the house. He walks beside me, neither of us saying anything.

I'm not sure where he wants to go. Maybe, he found another property he likes better. Maybe, he just wants to take me to have the breakup talk, so I don't make a scene in front of anyone like I'm one of *those* girls.

As the house comes back into view, you can tell everyone is starting to wake up. Some amazing smells are coming from the kitchen. Bacon, coffee, and heated syrup fill the air and mix with the hay and barn smell that has become so comforting to me here.

Mike opens his truck door for me, and I climb up, careful not to brush against him. He gives me a sad look and opens his mouth like he wants to say something. I turn to look straight ahead and see him give a slow nod, before closing my door.

He gets in and cranks the truck on to get the heat going, and Elvis singing "White Christmas" fills the truck.

A smile spreads across my face before I can stop it. "This is one of my favorites." I don't say any more and neither of us talk on the drive into town.

When we turn down the road to head towards Hunter's parents' house, I sit up straight but still say nothing. I can see Mike is tense too, so I figure I will just let this play out and see what he says.

He turns on to our driveway and drives past the main house down to the barn, before parking the truck.

"When I was here yesterday, I wasn't really here. I was blocking it all out, because I didn't want to get attached to the place, knowing it had already sold. Will you show it to me again?"

Hope starts to blossom in my heart, as we spend the next hour, walking through the barn, bunkhouses, and outbuildings, making plans.

As we walk back to his truck, I tell him about Wolf. "I had a contractor come out and give estimates of getting the work done on each building. It's the contractor Blaze and Sage used on the ranch. He's from the reservation and a really nice guy. Wolf is his name. I have the paperwork back at the house."

He helps me back into the truck, and we drive back up to the main house, but this time there are lights on covering the front porch.

"Mike, what did you do?" I gasp.

"It needed some Christmas decorations." He shrugs, as we get out and head inside the house. There's a tree all set up in what would be in the living room, giving a soft glow around the room.

I watch him walk around the main living areas, taking it all in like he's seeing it for the first time. When he finally looks back at me, he holds his hand out to me. My legs move against my will, and before I know it, I'm standing right in front of him.

"Over the last year, my dream has changed." He squeezes my hand, before continuing, "It changed from me working a ranch alone to working it with you. Yesterday, that dream changed again. I snapped because I didn't get to be part of the closing process on this place. Last night, I realized that didn't matter because all I could see was us living here and working here together. I always thought it would be me buying the place and trying to convince you to want to be here full-time. You shocked me and overwhelmed me yesterday, and I acted horribly. For that, I'm so sorry."

He takes a deep breath and then drops to one knee.

"I can't promise it won't happen again, and I can't promise we won't fight. I hope we do. I don't want to ever not work things out with you. I can promise I will love you with everything in my heart, and I will do everything in my power to make you happy. I would be honored to work this ranch with you by my side, as my wife. But if you have other dreams, I'll support those too, always. I don't want this life without you. Will you marry me?"

He pulls a ring from his pocket, and it's a beautiful vintage setting and prettier than anything I could have ever picked out myself. Everything starts to blur, as the tears fill my eyes and run down my face.

The man I want to spend the rest of my life with is down on one knee and has just laid his heart on the line. It's better than any wedding proposal I could have ever dreamed of.

"Yes!" I choke out, and a blinding smile lights up his face. He slides the ring on my finger, before standing up and pulling me into his arms.

"Look up, firecracker." He whispers in my ear. Looking up, I notice mistletoe. He just proposed to me under the mistletoe!

I laugh and pull him down for a kiss. A mistletoe kiss that still sends shocks down my whole body. A kiss that's the start of my forever.

Chapter 25

Mike

On the way home, I can't stop smiling. Lilly is pressed up to my side in the truck. Thank God for bench seats. Her hand in mine and the huge smile on her face allows me to breathe again, knowing everything is okay. We make plans for the house and ranch, as we drive home.

We walk in the door, and you could cut the tension with a knife. Something is wrong, we can feel it. I catch Blaze's attention first.

"Sage just got a call from the sheriff. A horse was dropped off at the church and it's drugged and has been abused badly. They think it's from that illegal rodeo. Though, they normally kill the horses and dump them, so we can't be sure. They called Sage for help and to see if we can board it."

"Well, why don't we board it at our place? It will be our first horse." Lilly says to me, and the room goes dead quiet. Not even the baby dares to make a noise.

"Your place?" Megan asks. Sage looks like she already knows what's going on, which I'm guessing she heard from Colt.

Even in the midst of the news about the horse, a smile spreads across my face.

"Lilly bought the place next to Hunter's parents and surprised me with it. Today, I asked her to marry me, and she said yes." I say.

Lilly holds up her hand, and all the girls squeal and run over to hug her and see the ring.

The guys come up to shake my hand and congratulate me.

"We still have some work to do on the place, so I'll be here for a bit. Gives you time to find my replacement," I say to Colt.

"We already know who will replace you. If we promote from within, we just have to hire a new ranch hand, and those are pretty easy to find," Colt says and pats my back.

"Okay, expect wedding talk later," Sage says, taking control of the situation. "Are you sure you can take on this horse?"

"Yes. We have to stop at the feed store to pick up a few things, but the barn and fences are all in good shape. Lilly said Wolf had been out there the same day as the inspector to go over everything," I tell them, and Mac smiles.

I know it means a lot to him that we work with guys from his reservation. Not everyone in town will. Even though he grew up here, he never turned his back on the tribe, and he has gone out of his way to smooth things over with those in town.

"Well, why doesn't he come here for a few days, until you get the barn set up, and then we can move him there after Christmas," Sage says.

Lilly and I agree with her.

"Okay, let's get the trailer hooked up. Hunter, you coming?"

"Yes, my dad is already on his way there, since he's closer. Jason and Mac will stay with the girls." Hunter says.

Hunter's dad is also a vet, but he's on his way to retiring and taking on less work at the clinic. Yet, he's always ready to jump in on emergencies like this.

"Let's go." I nod. Sage, Blaze, and Colt get the trailer hooked up and load up in the truck. Hunter rides with Lilly and me in my truck.

On the way, Hunter relays the info his dad texts him and gives us a rundown of what to expect. From the sounds of it, this horse is in pretty bad shape.

As we near the church, there's a flurry of activity. County and state police cars are blocking off the area in front of the church, and just about everyone in town is gathered around the barrier. Sage inches in with the trailer, and the crowd parts for her.

"Let's park over here and walk in," Hunter suggests. I park on the side of the street and help Lilly from the truck. I tuck her into my side, as we follow Hunter in.

"Hunter, your dad said you were coming with Sage." Shane, the sheriff, says, as he ushers us to the front of the church.

As we get our first look at the horse, Lilly gasps, and my heart skips a beat. I know animal abuse is out there, and I've seen some of it firsthand. It's what has driven my desire to rescue horses and other animals on our ranch. Nothing I've seen could have prepared me for the animal in front of me.

How this poor creature is still standing, I will never know. He's so skinny you can see every bone in his body. There are open and infected cuts all over his skin and scars where a few have healed over.

"Why is he so calm?" Lilly asks.

"It's the drugs. He feels nothing right now. Won't be the case once they wear off." Hunter says and then rushes to his dad's side.

"I'm so glad Riley didn't come with us," Blaze says, as he walks up beside us.

"Yes, but there will be no hiding him once he's at the ranch." I remind him.

He nods, as we walk over to where Hunter and his dad are.

"Look here, they cut the microchip out, and they weren't nice about it. Some of these slashes are from a whip, and some are burns." Hunter says as he takes stock of the injuries.

"All four legs are swollen, and he might not be able to stand, once the drugs wear off. I'm going to pull some blood samples now because we'll have to give him something for the ride back to the clinic. We can't chance whatever is in his system wearing off, until after we get him settled." Hunter's dad, Hank, says.

"Some of these cuts are badly infected, and I need to clean them before we try to load him. I've got some antibiotics we can give him, too." Hunter says as they keep working on him.

"What are the chances he survives?" I ask.

"I can't give a straight answer until we know what's in his system, and he comes out of it. If we can get the infection under control, and his legs aren't fractured, then it will be a long road, but he could recover. We need to get him to the clinic first, do some X-rays, and get him rehydrated. Then, we can go from there." Hank tells me.

"Lilly, come with me," Sage says softly and takes Lilly's hand. They make their way around to the front of the horse, where he's tied to the church handrail. Sage shows Lilly some calming methods, and they begin talking to the horse.

Shane comes to stand next to me. "Sage says you and Lilly are willing to take this guy in once cleared?"

"Yes, we bought the ranch next to Hank's, and our plan is to take in abused and abandoned horses and give them a new life. We want to have a summer camp for kids to work with horses. I went to a camp like that as a kid, and it changed me. It kept me out of trouble and gave me a goal in life."

"I'm happy to help any way I can. I'll add your name with Sage's to call in events like this. Sometimes, a horse is found wandering on the side of the road, and the owner comes to claim them, but Sage has gotten a few good horses that have never been claimed."

"What about this guy? If he had a microchip, he must have been reported missing." I ask. He is black all over with several distinct white markings, so he should be easy to identify.

"I went over the reports just before you got here, nothing matching his description. The state police have been looking over their files too and nothing. Chances are with the scars it looks like they have been using this horse for a while. The owner will have collected insurance on it, and in this condition, won't want it back."

I shake my head. I can't fathom tossing a horse to the side. One who was part of your family, and simply because some cruel people hurt him, and now, he requires care. He needs love more than ever now.

I do know this cruelty will make it hard for him to trust people now, especially any of us. He doesn't know us, and he's trained to think people he doesn't know will hurt him. But we will earn his trust back and spoil him for the rest of his days with us.

"Do you think this is from that illegal rodeo?" I ask him.

"I'd say I'm 99.99% sure it is. Though, this is the first time any of us have seen a horse come out of it alive. We normally just find them shot dead in a ditch somewhere."

"Any idea why they left this one alive?"

"If I had to put my money on anything, it would be one of the low on the totem pole guys had a heart and couldn't kill him, so they dumped him here to get help. He has a clean conscience, and no one else knows. Why they chose here could be a million reasons from they know the area, or they just randomly drove through and anything in between."

Shane walks off, and Hank joins me at the same time Blaze does.

"Hunter tells me you and Lilly bought the ranch next door and plan to rescue horses on it?" Hank asks.

"Yes sir," I reply.

"I'm semi-retired and help in the office a few days a week. I'd be honored to be your vet on the ranch when you get cases like this or even day-to-day things. My wife and I used to rescue all kinds of animals. She still does, but mostly dogs now. It's always been a passion of ours, and we'd be happy to help you in any way we can." Hank says.

"I'll take you up on that. Hunter did tell me of a time you had a monkey that was dropped off at your clinic." I laugh.

"Yes, how about I tell you all about it over lunch next week. We can iron out all the details." He shakes my hand.

"Sounds good. I'll get with you after we know what's going on with this guy." I nod towards the horse.

It's still another twenty minutes before Hunter looks at me. "Okay, I just gave him some medication, so let's get him in the trailer and to the clinic, so we can get some X-rays before it wears off."

The next few hours are a flurry of activity transporting the horse to the clinic, getting X-rays, and treatment plans done. Treating more of his open wounds and sores and stitching a few up.

"Mom and Dad are going to stay with him tonight and do their Christmas here at the clinic," Hunter says, as we head out to the truck. "He has a hairline fracture in his right front leg, and we're shocked that's the only fracture he has. If we can keep him calm coming out of the drug haze, then he has a chance to heal it. Dad has him on an IV to get him hydrated again, and he ate a little bit of food. The next few days will tell what kind of chance he has. Dad also called in a special favor at the lab, and we'll know in a few hours what's in his system." Hunter says.

On the way home, we make plans on what we will need to take care of him at the ranch, along with other items we need to stock and should have on hand. As soon as we walk in the door, the questions start, and Hunter takes over telling the whole story.

Riley, Megan, and Ella have tears in their eyes, as Hunter describes how the horse was treated. I pull Lilly upstairs to her old room and close the door behind me.

"You still in this, firecracker? There could be days worse than this. We won't be able to save every animal, no matter how hard we try. You still want to do this?"

"100%. Standing there with him today, while Hunter and Hank were working on him, I knew this is where I was meant to be. There isn't a bit of doubt in me."

I pull her close and kiss her, conveying everything I feel and can't put into words. As her soft lips move gently across mine, I tangle my hands in her hair and deepen the kiss.

Her body melts against mine, and I know at that moment, I agree with her. This is exactly where we both belong.

She pulls away slightly and with a glazed look in her eyes.

"I think we should call him Black Diamond. He looked at me, and even in the drug haze, his eyes shined like diamonds." She whispers.

"Well, he's officially family now that you've named him. Let's go join the others."

It's not a traditional Christmas by any means, but it's ours. It's a Christmas filled with family, friends, surprises, mistletoe, and love. What more can you ask for?

Epilogue

I'm at WJ's helping my sister Ella take down the Christmas decor and decorating for the New Year's party they are going to have. They have done some great things turning this bar into a family dining spot. I think a huge part of that is, because of Nick and his food.

Ella has been great about capitalizing on the fame from Nick's BBQ championship win in Dallas. It's been good for the whole town.

"Penny for your thoughts?" Ella joins me in wrapping up decorations, as we box them up.

"Just thinking about everything you and Jason have done with this place. I know Mom and Dad were hesitant about it, but I want you to know how proud of you I am."

"Ahhh," Ella suddenly hugs me. "I want you to know I support you. I know you want to be more independent than I was. I think you'll do great with the photography. Jason and I will sit down with you when you talk to Mom and Dad."

"I don't know. I asked them at dinner last night about wearing jeans, instead of skirts and dresses. I think I shocked them. It's a practical thing, and they're better than dresses and leggings. I hope they'll get on board with it, instead of making me go against them, but I decided I'm going to do it, regardless."

Growing up, Mom and Dad insisted us girls only wear skirts and dresses. I never knew anything else, and since we would wear leggings under them, it has never been a problem.

Then, we came to the ranch, and the more time we spend here, the more I'm seeing how practical jeans are. Not just as pants, but they offer more protection from the elements on the ranch and while riding horses. I agree with Mom and Dad's views on dressing modestly and what should be covered, and I won't change that. I'd just like to wear jeans instead.

"Maybe, I'll let the shock of that conversation wear off, before talking about the photography," I say hesitantly.

"Well, I'll be there regardless, just let me know when."

I nod and try for a subject change.

"Any more on that horse that was dropped off?" I ask her.

It's been about a week now since the horse had been left in front of the church.

"Well, they named him Black Diamond, and he's gained some weight and is eating well. He's in a lot of pain, so he's been on medication. They've kept him at the clinic, but Lilly thinks he might be able to go home next week. They went out the day after Christmas and bought everything they needed and got a stall ready for him."

"Are Mike and Lilly going to live at the ranch, once Black Diamond is there?"

"Yeah, they decided to stay in the foreman's house, while they renovate the main house, so they can be close to the barn. They have some guys there now doing the work on the barn. A new roof and fixing a few stalls, I think." Ella pauses in thought. "I know they wanted the barn done, before Black Diamond got out there, as they aren't sure if the noise would affect him."

"He's really skittish, isn't he?"

"Can you blame the poor guy? He doesn't know who to trust. Once he's healed, Mike said he'll work with him and gain his trust back no matter how long it takes."

Mike is a good guy, and I think he and Lilly will do great with their new ranch.

"Any word on their wedding?" I ask Ella.

"Well, Sage offered them the old church on the ranch where everyone else was married this year, but Lilly says she wants to get married on their land, so we girls are all going out there tomorrow to start making plans. You should come with us and give us an idea of what will work with photos."

"I'd like that. I want to see the place, too."

After we are finished packing up the Christmas decorations, I decide to get some fresh air.

"Hey Ella. I'm going to go for a walk, while we wait on Jason to get those New Year's decorations out of storage."

"Okay, take your time!" She calls back.

I decide to walk down Main Street and do some window shopping. There are so many really cute shops and antique stores here. A few new ones have popped up with all the business WJ's is now bringing to town.

It's nothing for people and families from Dallas to come for the day to eat at WJ's, do some shopping, and then head home. The town wants to do a few more events this upcoming summer to bring more people in for the weekend.

I'm staring at a window display of a new clothing shop selling some really cute boots when a hand is placed on my arm. I nearly jump out of my skin, as I turn to see Nick next to me.

"Sorry, I called your name, but you seemed lost in thought," he says.

"Yes, sorry lots on my mind. Taking a break from the decorations, while Jason puts the Christmas ones away and gets out the New Year's ones."

"Thank you for helping with that, by the way." He falls into step beside me, as we slowly walk back towards WJ's.

"It's fun spending time with my sister. We have always decorated together."

"I was wondering if you would like to go get dinner with me this weekend? There's a diner I've been wanting to try out about twenty minutes from here."

Is he asking me out on a date? I've never been out on a date. I've never even been asked out on a date, for that matter. I think it would really be too much for my parents to handle right now. Introducing things to them slowly, is the way to go.

I know I don't want to do courting the way Ella did, but I'm also pretty sure I'm not ready to date just yet either.

"I don't think that's a good idea." I cringe even hearing myself say the words. I wish I knew how to let him down easier than that. I do like Nick, and I think he's the kind of guy I would like to go on a date with at some point down the road.

"Well, with the holidays and all, it could be good to get a break from the craziness." He tries again.

I stop myself from smiling. It actually feels good to have a guy want to go out with you.

"It's not that." I hope he will drop it, but when he looks over at me, I know I'm not that lucky.

"Can I ask why, then?" He isn't being rude, he just sounds genuinely interested. Nick has been good to Jason and Ella, and I think I owe him the truth for that alone.

"I think telling my parents I'm going on a date would kill them right now. I'm trying to slowly break them into the life I want. To be more independent. I'm trying to figure out what that means for me, too."

We reach the bar, and he puts his arm out to stop me from opening the door.

"You'll figure that out with flying colors, but I'm not giving up so easy, Maggie." He leans in a bit closer. "You can count on it."

. . . • . • ● . • ● . • ● . . .

Get The Next Book in the Rock Springs Texas Series! Maggie and Nick's Story!
The Cowboy and His Valentine is Maggie and Nick's Story!

. . . . • . ● . • ● . • . . .

Would you like some free cowboy books?
If you join Kaci M. Rose's Newsletter you get books and bonus epilogues free!
Join Kaci M. Rose's newsletter and get your free books!
https://www.kacirose.com/KMR-Newsletter

Connect with Kaci M. Rose

Kaci M. Rose writes steamy small town cowboys. She also writes under Kaci Rose and there she writes wounded military heroes, giant mountain men, sexy rock stars, and even more there. Connect with her below!

Website
Facebook
Kaci Rose Reader's Facebook Group
Goodreads
Book Bub
Join Kaci M. Rose's VIP List (Newsletter)

More Books by Kaci M. Rose

Rock Springs Texas Series
The Cowboy and His Runaway – Blaze and Riley
The Cowboy and His Best Friend – Sage and Colt
The Cowboy and His Obsession – Megan and Hunter
The Cowboy and His Sweetheart – Jason and Ella
The Cowboy and His Secret – Mac and Sarah
Rock Springs Weddings Novella
Rock Springs Box Set 1-5 + Bonus Content

Cowboys of Rock Springs
The Cowboy and His Mistletoe Kiss – Lilly and Mike
The Cowboy and His Valentine – Maggie and Nick

The Cowboy and His Vegas Wedding – Royce and Anna
The Cowboy and His Angel – Abby and Greg
The Cowboy and His Christmas Rockstar – Savannah and Ford
The Cowboy and His Billionaire – Brice and Kayla

Walker Lake, Texas
The Cowboy and His Beauty - Sky and Dash

About Kaci M Rose

Kaci M Rose writes cowboy, hot and steamy cowboys set in all town anywhere you can find a cowboy.

She enjoys horseback riding and attending a rodeo where is always looking for inspiration.

Kaci grew on a small farm/ranch in Florida where they raised cattle and an orange grove. She learned to ride a four-wheeler instead of a bike (and to this day still can't ride a bike) and was driving a tractor before she could drive a car.

Kaci prefers the country to the city to this day and is working to buy her own slice of land in the next year or two!
Kaci M Rose is the Cowboy Romance alter ego of Author Kaci Rose.

See all of Kaci Rose's Books here.

Please Leave a Review!

I love to hear from my readers! Please **head over to your favorite store and leave a review** of what you thought of this book!

www.ingramcontent.com/pod-product-compliance
Lightning Source LLC
Chambersburg PA
CBHW071238190726
48292CB00007B/2345